THE TOUCH OF THISTLEDOWN

When Clare, a recently qualified solicitor, meets Neal on the way to her cousin's wedding in Suffolk, his arrogant views on a woman's place in the profession annoy her. Nevertheless, she finds herself reluctantly becoming very attracted to him, despite her involvement with a married partner in the firm where she works. Suffolk and Neal are never far from her life — or her heart; though when one of her clients makes an unexpected, desperate move, Clare finds she is fighting for her life as well as her future happiness.

REBECCA BENNETT

THE
TOUCH OF
THISTLEDOWN

Complete and Unabridged

LINFORD
Leicester

First published in Great Britain in 1990 by
Robert Hale Limited
London

First Linford Edition
published 2016
by arrangement with
Robert Hale Limited
London

A catalogue record for this book is available
from the British Library.

ISBN 978–1–4448–2800–9

Published by
F. A. Thorpe (Publishing)
Anstey, Leicestershire

Set by Words & Graphics Ltd.
Anstey, Leicestershire
Printed and bound in Great Britain by
T. J. International Ltd., Padstow, Cornwall

This book is printed on acid-free paper

1

There had to be enough time to draft out Miss Milsom's will before the train reached Suffolk. Clare forced her eyes over the closely-written notes she'd made earlier that afternoon, but the green and gold patchwork of fields racing past the window and the rhythmic swaying of the carriage made them blur. Weariness closed round her like a heavy enveloping cloak and within seconds her eyelids were beginning to droop.

* * *

It wasn't until something hot splashed onto the back of her hand that she jerked awake again suddenly.

'Sorry!' apologised a deep voice.

Concerned dark eyes were looking down at her from a tanned good-looking face. Two brimming plastic beakers wavered in his hands.

'I brought you a coffee — at least I think that's what it's meant to be,' he said, peering doubtfully into the cups. 'You look as if you need it.'

Clare sat up, pushing back the untidy tangle of auburn hair from her face, and glanced at her watch, horrified to find it was well over half an hour since the train had left London.

She smiled uncertainly back at him, still only half awake.

'I must have been . . . '

'You were,' he grinned, holding out a beaker. 'Deeply asleep — and snoring too. Very delicately though, may I hasten to add. Anyway, this'll soon perk you up a bit.'

Clare sipped the steaming liquid and gave a slight shudder at its bitterness.

'It is pretty awful, isn't it,' he laughed, accurately reading her thoughts for the second time.

With a relaxed movement he stretched out his long legs and leaned back against the seat. 'D'you live or

2

work in London?'

'Both,' Clare replied, carefully balancing the beaker in one hand as she tucked the notes back into her bag.

'I thought so. How can you bear it? It's such a terrible place! All that rush and fuss. A couple of hours there is quite enough for me.'

He studied her critically with his dark eyes. 'No wonder you're so washed-out and exhausted.'

Washed-out and exhausted! Clare stiffened angrily. Who on earth did he think he was?

'Towns sap all your energy, you know,' he continued blithely. 'They're full of poisonous toxic fumes, not to mention all those aggressive bodies pushing and shoving you around. That's what's making you so tired.'

Clare glared across the carriage at him, her green eyes hostile, but he seemed totally unaware of her annoyance.

'Do you know, every girl I've seen around London today looks like a zombie plodding along, all hunched up, face tight, eyes blank — just like you. You're typical.'

Trying to ignore his remarks, Clare stared fixedly out of the window. Her gaunt, hollow-eyed reflection stared back, mirrored by the growing darkness outside. She looked away quickly. Perhaps he was right after all.

'Thank you for the coffee,' she said with chill politeness, hoping to indicate an end to their conversation.

His dark-brown eyes were instantly apologetic. 'Please don't take offence. I didn't mean it to be taken personally, you know. It's just that you seem to be a classic example of the modern woman. One of that fast-growing breed: the independent-liberated-every-man-should-be-exterminated-career-minded female.'

'Are you deliberately being insulting?' she snapped.

'No, merely honest. It's true though, isn't it?' he replied with a broad smile. 'What's your job?'

'I really can't see why it should be of

any interest to you, but if you must know, I'm a solicitor.'

'All slime, crimes and dimes.'

'I beg your pardon?' Ice glazed her voice.

'Divorce, robbery, assault, murder, bankruptcy . . . ' he explained. 'That's what your work consists of, doesn't it? Are you any good?'

Clare hesitated for a second before answering, then her chin tipped upwards.

'I think so. I usually win my cases,' she said stiffly.

'And do you find it hard, competing in a man's world?'

'A man's world! It's not a man's world,' she retorted furiously. 'Women are just as good, if not better, solicitors.'

'Are they?' he questioned. 'But don't you find you become emotionally involved? The deserted wife? That mugged old lady? Don't you relate to them? Don't they pull at your heart-strings far more than they would a man's?' He smiled wryly at the look on her face. 'Oh, for goodness sake, don't get all uptight again. I'm just curious. I always thought women were basically much softer creatures than men. Forgive me if I'm wrong. Maybe it's just the kind I meet.'

'You're allowed your opinion, I suppose — even if it is a biased one,' Clare replied coldly.

'Based on observation and fact, m'lud,' he mocked.

'Having been forced to listen to your bigoted views, now may I state mine?' she commented in a scathing tone. 'You are a typical chauvinist male, unable to accept that any woman can do a job as well, if not better, than a man.'

'Not at all,' he replied, settling himself more comfortably against the back of the seat as if to enjoy the argument more fully, his knee brushing hers as he did so.

'I accept that a woman can do the job equally well, but I wonder at what cost? That's what really concerns me.'

He gave her an appraising look before continuing: 'Mentally and physically, what does it do to her — this task of keeping up, trying to be even better? Seeing you, sitting there all white-faced, tense and taut, sharp and prickly, only makes me wonder even more.'

Angrily Clare pulled Miss Milsom's notes from her bag and began to read them, her eyes travelling the same lines over and over again, but nothing settled into her brain. She was far too aware of the dark-eyed gaze watching her across the carriage with unconcealed amusement.

If she hadn't agreed to be Nicola's bridesmaid, she wouldn't now be suffering his pompous remarks. She closed her eyes, trying to shut him out of her mind, and leaned her head against the seat, remembering that wretched letter that started the whole thing off.

★   ★   ★

'Oh no, not another wedding,' she groaned, opening the flower-strewn envelope.

7

Why on earth did people bother? Surely they must know the end result? Unhappiness, misery, constant battles, that was their destiny. Clare saw it happening every day of her life. She spent a great deal of time in her job sorting out the tangled threads of bitter, ruined marriages. Now marriage was something she wouldn't ever think of for herself.

Slowly she read her cousin's letter. Every line was bursting with happiness and excitement. It filled each sentence with such enthusiasm that Clare could only despair.

Nicola had known John ever since he came to teach at the same school as she did, near her home in Suffolk. Two whole years. It had been instant attraction — for both of them. Love at first sight, she enthused. And now, they were getting married.

Clare sighed. How could they be so foolish? Why spoil a perfectly good relationship? Two intelligent people like that. But then, Nicky always had

8

been a romantic.

'You *will* be my bridesmaid, won't you?' the letter ended.

No way, thought Clare. She hadn't the time — nor the inclination. With her current workload, she was far too busy even to go to the wedding, let alone be a bridesmaid. It would mean travelling all the way up to Suffolk and probably spending the whole weekend there. She really couldn't manage that.

Once, nothing would have given her more pleasure. Over the years she'd been bridesmaid to two of her mother's younger sisters, three of the neighbours' daughters and one of her own friends. She had a row of useless, never-to-be-worn-again dresses half-filling her wardrobe.

What does one do with a bridesmaid's dress after the event? It's too elaborate for a dance and far too beautiful to give to a jumble-sale; so there they hung, glazed in plastic bags, taking up much-needed space.

Nicky was different though. Once,

they'd been almost like sisters. Both only children; her cousin living by the sea in Suffolk; Clare's mother divorced and working all the time, only too pleased for her small daughter to spend every summer holiday there.

Life had been wonderful then, roaming the beach together, every day carefree and a challenge; collecting shells, pressing strands of seaweed into scrap-books, learning to swim, then to windsurf and sail. They'd been so close as children.

But as time passed, their interests changed and they'd grown apart. Nicola went to Reading University and eventually became a history teacher, while Clare took up law.

They hadn't met for at least six or seven years. There was the occasional letter, usually at Christmas or birthdays, catching up on events, but the news of Nicola's wedding had come quite out of the blue.

In the end Clare decided, rather reluctantly, she would have to go, whatever her workload. Now that her mother was living with her new husband in America, someone had to represent the family — and there wasn't anyone else.

She wrote back accepting and, as an afterthought, added: 'Come down to London one Saturday, Nicky, and we can choose your dress.'

★ ★ ★

It was a chilly May morning when Nicola arrived, the stark, bare trees lining the roads and in the parks only just breaking into leaf, after a long cold winter which had extended well into what should have been spring.

After more than six years Clare wondered whether she would recognise her cousin again. Nicky had been a plump and noisy teenager when they last met, all giggles and wayward hair that frizzled over her head in a riot of tawny curls.

'Clare!'

She turned at the sound of that familiar breathless voice — and stared in amazement. Surely this tall, slender girl couldn't be Nicola? That beautiful hair swept up into a rich sleek coil at the back of her head; those enormous dark-fringed grey eyes; that perfect glowing golden skin? She looked like a glamorous model in an expensive glossy magazine advertisement.

'Nicky! What a transformation!'

Instantly two arms closed warmly round her, hugging her, and Clare laughed with delight, knowing her cousin hadn't changed at all. Nicky always had been an impulsive, affectionate child, hugging and kissing everyone as if they'd been to the ends of the earth and back.

'Well, you've changed!' her cousin replied, stepping back and frowning slightly as she studied Clare from top to toe. 'It took me a minute or two to recognise you at all. Do you always dress so severely? You used to be such a blaze of colour with that flame-coloured hair and way-out brilliant dresses. You made me feel dreadfully dowdy.'

Clare glanced down at the black suit she was wearing.

'I don't bother with casual clothes any more. There's never time to wear them. And it has to be dark colours for court work.'

'But today's Saturday,' protested Nicola. 'You're not going to court.'

'Oh come on, Nicky,' Clare laughed, seizing her arm. 'Don't start lecturing me the minute we meet. I'd forgotten you were such a little bossy-boots. That's one thing that hasn't changed. No wonder you're a school-teacher. Let's find somewhere for coffee, then we'll start looking for a wedding-dress for you.'

* * *

With her lovely figure, everything Nicola tried on looked fabulous. The choice was going to be difficult, but one was perfect on her — a closely-fitting ivory silk with low scalloped neck that showed off her creamy skin to perfection, then clung to her body before swirling out in a full skirt, sweeping behind into a long train.

'It has to be that one,' Clare insisted, seeing the expression on her cousin's face and knowing she felt the same way.

Nicola shook her head. 'I can't, Clare. It's far too expensive. John and I are on a pretty tight budget, what with the house and everything.'

Regretfully she began to undo the tiny buttons fastening the sleeves.

'You're having it.' Clare's voice was firm. 'It can be my wedding-present to you. I really have no idea what to give you and this will solve the problem nicely.'

Nicola's grey eyes swam with instant tears. 'No, Clare. I couldn't do that. It's much too much.'

Without another word, Clare produced her bank card and handed it to the plump middle-aged assistant who was standing, staring from one girl to the other, waiting for their decision with a slight frown of impatience.

'No more arguments, Nicky. You're having it and that's final. And for goodness sake don't worry about the money. My salary is ridiculous in any case — so it's good to be able to spend it on something worthwhile. Now, how are you going to wear your hair on the day?'

'Oh, up. It's much tidier. Remember what a ghastly frizz it gets into otherwise? I look like something that's been dragged through a hedge — several times — backwards.'

'Then how about this,' Clare suggested, picking up a tiara-style headdress, and was delighted to see how well it suited the other girl, resting on her thick upswept hair most regally, making her look like a princess.

'And now we have to sort you out,' said Nicola, while the dress was being packed into an enormous box, her eyes taking in the gaunt angular figure and colourless skin of her cousin.

15

'You've got so thin, Clare. It's not going to be easy. What style and colour do you fancy?'

'It's really up to you,' Clare replied with a non-committal shrug. 'I haven't the slightest clue about fashion any more. What's the point? Black, grey or navy are my everyday colours nowadays.'

Nicola stared at her critically. 'You're awfully pale, you know. Don't you ever wear any make-up?'

Clare shook her head. 'No, Nicky, I don't. I really haven't the time to waste messing about with it.'

'Well, you need something to lift that pallid complexion a little,' her cousin replied firmly. 'Let's try some blusher.'

She produced a make-up pouch from her bag, laughing as Clare backed swiftly away.

'Oh, come on, Clare. Be fair. It's no use trying on these dresses without looking right — and you really do look like a ghost.'

Even with a touch of colour to her

face and smudge of lipstick, none of the outfits seemed to suit her and as the time wore on, Clare grew more and more despondent.

I used to look quite pretty, so what's changed? she thought, staring at herself in the mirror. Nicola's right. I am thin.

Meals were something she didn't bother about all that much. There was a convenient Indian take-away on the corner of the street and she'd buy something as she rushed home, pop it into the microwave and eat it with one hand while she made notes about a client with the other.

Beside Nicola's suntanned and glowing face, hers was pale and sharp-boned, her eyes lustreless and ringed by dark shadows, her once bright hair limp, brushing the collar of her dark jacket in untidy straggles.

With a shock she suddenly realised what a wreck she was turning into. No, she corrected herself, that's wrong — have already turned into. Nicola looked years younger and yet they were both the same age.

I don't have time to spend on myself, Clare thought defensively, not if I want to get anywhere with my career. It was hard work, fighting the prejudices of clients when it came to a woman representing them. She had to be good — and shown to be too.

'How about this one?' Nicola's voice broke through her reverie and Clare saw she was holding up a deep sea-green silk dress, somewhat similar in style to her own. 'It's a fantastic shade.'

Clare looked doubtful.

'It's a bit bright, isn't it?' she queried, but the effect was better on than off, the richness of the colour heightening the delicacy of her skin and making her red hair appear quite striking.

It fitted perfectly, too, so there would be no need, she decided, to waste hours coming back for alterations.

'What do you think?' she asked Nicola.

'Well, it's the best we've seen on you,

so we'd better have it,' her cousin replied wearily, and Clare glanced sharply at her, wondering whether Nicola was beginning to regret having asked her to be bridesmaid.

*   *   *

Leaving all the packages at the shop to be collected later in the day, the two girls spent the afternoon at a matinée. It was a long time since Clare had been to the theatre and although the play Nicola chose was a light and zany piece of nonsense, she enjoyed it. Her cousin's natural enthusiasm and infectious laughter soon had her feeling relaxed and joining in fits of giggles, just like the old days when they'd been children at the cinema together.

After a meal and loaded with bulging carrier bags, they walked through the grey twilit streets to the station, in plenty of time for Nicola to catch the train back to Suffolk.

'You've changed, you know, Clare,'

Nicola commented ruefully. 'You were always such fun to be with.'

'Fun!' Clare retorted sharply. 'Oh, come on, Nicky. We all have to grow up. That was years ago. You can't go on being silly and frivolous for ever, can you? Anyway, there's not much fun in life, is there? I find most of it's depressing and sordid.'

Nicola's grey eyes widened as she stared back at her.

'Is it? Yours may be, I suppose — with the kind of job you do — but surely it doesn't have to be like that. What do you do in your spare time? You never come up to visit us any more. Where do you go for your holidays?'

'Spare time! Holidays! You must be joking.'

'But Clare, you can't work all the time. What about boyfriends? You always had a string of them trailing after you. I used to be terribly jealous.'

Boyfriends, thought Clare, remembering. They were something she'd given up years ago, realising at university that if she wanted a good degree, she'd have to devote all her time to work. Then, after that, there'd been law school and now . . .

There was Geoffrey, of course — not exactly a boyfriend — but no way could she tell Nicola about him. Not yet.

'Isn't there anyone?' Nicola persisted.

'You'll miss your train if you don't hurry,' Clare said, quickly diverting the conversation.

'John will go frantic if I do,' her cousin laughed. 'He'll be waiting at the station to drive me home.'

'He sounds nice.'

Nicola had done nothing but talk about him on and off all day.

'He is nice,' her cousin replied, her face lighting up — and suddenly Clare envied her.

Doors slammed and the whistle blew.

'See you in three weeks then.'

Nicola's hand was still waving as the train swayed out of the station and disappeared into the hazy distance.

* ★ ★

'Shall I get your case down? We'll be arriving any second now.'

The man's deep voice broke into her thoughts.

Clare opened her eyes to stare back at him across the carriage.

'Or isn't that kind of thing allowed — you being such an independent young lady?' There was a note of mockery now.

Clare pointedly ignored him and rose to her feet, lifting down the expensive leather bag and dumping it on the floor.

As the train stopped, she stepped out onto the platform to be seized in Nicola's arms and kissed enthusiastically on both cheeks.

'Oh good, you've already met Neal, John's best man,' her cousin observed, turning her head to smile a welcome at the tall man climbing down from the carriage behind them.

He bowed, grinning wickedly at Clare.

'Ah,' he said, his eyes twinkling with mischief. 'So that's who you are. Nicky's long-lost cousin Clare. Well, well, well. From what I've heard about you, I'd never have guessed. What a surprise!'

2

'Put her suitcase in the boot, there's a dear, Neal,' said Nicola.

'Dare I?' He looked at Clare with a barely hidden glimmer of laughter. 'Or will it cause offence?'

'Stop teasing, Neal,' she commanded in a very school-mistressly tone, eyeing them both curiously. 'Why on earth should it cause offence? And do hurry up. Mum and Dad are dying to see Clare again. Are you coming back with us or did you leave your car here?'

'No, John dropped me off this morning, so I'd be only too pleased of a lift, Nicky, although how I'm going to concertina myself into that wretched little tin box of yours, I hate to think.'

Neal grimaced as he opened the door of Nicola's Mini and squeezed himself into the back seat, while Clare settled herself more comfortably in the front.

She was very aware of the long-limbed man behind her, smelling the faint masculine scent of his aftershave and the tweed of his jacket as he rested one arm on the back of her seat, his head bent to prevent it hitting the roof, so that his chin lightly touched her hair with every jolt.

The car rattled and bumped its way along the narrow lanes across stretches of open moorland. Nothing has changed, Clare thought, gazing through the window at the countryside speeding by. The trees, the river winding its way through marshland down to the sea, the tall water-towers rising here and there. Nothing has changed.

Only me.

Suddenly and unexpectedly, as always happened, the town came into view, clustered along the edge of the sea, the uneven roofs of the houses silhouetted against the night sky. There was such a quiet, tranquil air about it, unspoilt and untouched by the passing years as if in a different century.

With an abrupt jerk that threw them forward, so that Neal's face came alarmingly close to Clare's, Nicola pulled up outside a tall Victorian house bordered by a smooth well-kept green. Having been watching from the window for their arrival, her parents were already hurrying down the path, their faces full of welcome.

'Clare! And Neal too. Did you get the suits all right, dear?' Aunt Margaret asked anxiously, bending to speak to him through the open door of the car.

Neal unwound himself from the back seat to undo the boot and Clare saw the huge cardboard box he had stowed in there with her case before they left the station.

'Our wedding outfits,' he whispered to her with a hint of mischief. 'We men have to be equal to the females these days, you know. Can't let you wear all the finery.'

Clare ignored his teasing words and hugged Aunt Margaret, noticing the concerned expression as her aunt's eyes studied her.

'You look so tired, dear. Quite peaky, in fact. What you need is a few days of peace and quiet here with us.'

Neal raised his eyebrows and smiled slightly but for once made no comment, which surprised Clare. Surely this was a good opportunity for him to announce that he agreed with her aunt entirely — and make her feel even worse?

'You will stop and have supper with us, won't you, Neal?' Aunt Margaret said, hurrying them all up the path. 'John's here.'

'Thanks, I'd love to, then I can prove to him I've collected the right suits. He's been going frantic in case his turns out to be too big or his topper won't fit — not that any of them do. Only guys with big ears can cope with those properly.'

He seems just as much a part of the family as John, Clare decided, watching Neal settle himself down at the table, chatting easily to Uncle Bill and passing round plates and cups of tea with relaxed ease.

Unfortunately she was placed directly opposite him and found his gaze disconcerting as she began to fill her plate from the many bowls of salad and side dishes.

'Take plenty, dear,' encouraged Aunt Margaret. 'You need a lot more flesh on those bones. I've never seen such a change in anyone. You're like a skeleton.'

Clare refused to meet Neal's taunting eyes and turned her attention to Nicola and John as they sat side by side, so close they could easily have used one chair.

'Should you two be together? I thought it was unlucky for the bride and groom to meet.'

'That's not until tomorrow, before the actual ceremony — isn't it?' Nicola's grey eyes were suddenly anxious, turning to question her mother.

'Of course it is, dear,' Aunt Margaret soothed.

'Then it's lucky we're getting married early in the morning,' said John, bending to kiss the upturned face next to him. 'I couldn't bear to keep away from you for too long.'

Neal's dark eyes met Clare's with a look of amusement and she felt her cheeks burn, realising her envious feelings must have shown plainly on her own face as she stared at the couple who were so obviously deeply in love. But was she wrong to imagine she'd recognised envy in his own eyes when he, too, looked at Nicky and John?

'How long are you staying?' he asked her as if aware of her unspoken question and wishing to distract her.

'I'm travelling back straight after the ceremony.'

'Oh no!' cried Aunt Margaret. 'You must stay longer than that, Clare. Can't you go back on Sunday evening or even Monday? It's been such a time since we saw you. Surely you can spare us a little longer than that, dear.'

'Well . . . ' Already the tranquillity that surrounded the peaceful little town was lulling her and she felt very tempted to stay on.

'I've got so much work to do, Aunt Margaret . . . '

'And you'll do it all far better after a break away for a couple of days,' declared her aunt firmly.

'Well, perhaps until Sunday then — if you don't mind.'

'Of course we don't mind. It's going to be very quiet without Nicola around. We'd be only too pleased to have you here to make a fuss of instead,' Uncle Bill confessed in his mild voice, before retiring hastily behind his newspaper again, as if fearing he'd said too much.

'That's it then. You're staying,' announced Aunt Margaret.

And there wasn't any more to be said on the subject after that.

★ ★ ★

Through her open bedroom window that night Clare could hear the sea sigh softly a few yards away and breathe the fragrant smell of roses and lavender mingled with the salt air. She stood, gazing out into the velvety darkness, seeing the faint glimmer of stars high above — something rarely seen in the bright streetlights of her own London home — feeling the tension slowly slip away from her. All her problems, all her worries, had already vanished.

Somehow nothing seemed to matter any more. Not here.

She slept deeply, dreaming of a church filled with flowers, their heady perfume filling the air; walking down a long and endless aisle and seeing, standing there far in the distance, a tall hazy figure, waiting. And then, when at last she reached his side, he turned and smiled. A wicked teasing smile that lit his dark eyes and tilted his wide mouth delightfully at the corners . . .

⋆　⋆　⋆

A slight mist hung over the sea, blurring the skyline, when Clare woke.

'That means a fine day,' Aunt Margaret assured her, glancing out of the window as she bustled in with a cup of tea. 'Now you stay in bed as long as you like, dear. There's no need at all for you to get up yet and you look as if you could do with a rest.'

She twitched back the curtains a little further, carefully straightening their edges.

'You're working too hard, you know, Clare. It always shows on the face first.'

Do I really look that dreadful? Clare wondered. And yet, seeing Nicky aglow with excitement, she knew there was no comparison. I used to be the pretty one — years back, she thought, but maybe love produced that kind of radiance.

Why then wasn't she radiant too? Why didn't she look like that — as if a fire was burning somewhere deep within her? Didn't she love Geoffrey?

Maybe things would change when Geoffrey was free . . .

But would he ever be free? Did he really want to be? Sometimes she doubted it. There was always some excuse. The boys were too young to desert. Eileen, his wife, wouldn't be able to cope without him.

And yet he said he loved and wanted only her.

'What you need is a husband to take care of you, Clare,' Aunt Margaret was saying. 'Surely you must have some nice young man back there in London?'

Should she tell her? Ask her advice? Aunt Margaret had always been the one to listen to her troubles, never her mother. She was always too busy. But Aunt Margaret was different.

'There is someone . . . ' she began, but at that moment the doorbell rang and her aunt hurried away down the stairs to answer it.

Seconds later Nicola appeared, her long tawny hair a riot of curls cascading nearly to her waist when she danced into the room, wearing an old pair of flowered pyjamas and looking about twelve years old as she hunched herself under the duvet on Clare's bed, hugging her knees to her chin.

'Two more hours,' she uttered in her breathless voice. 'Two more hours and I'll be Mrs John Maxwell.'

'You really love him so much?'

'So much,' Nicola murmured dreamily.

'What does being in love feel like?' Clare asked curiously.

Nicola's face was thoughtful for a second, then she smiled.

'It's as if I'm floating — like thistledown — all light and fluffy, about to burst. Oh, I don't know how to explain it. But I do know I can't live without John. Without him, life has nothing for me at all. He is my life, Clare.'

The grey eyes were enormous, filled with a luminous intensity that seemed to reach every corner of the room. Then they clouded, brimming with sudden tears. 'All I hope is he feels the same about me, but how does one ever know, Clare?'

'No doubts, not today, Nicky,' her cousin insisted.

'How do I know it will last, Clare?'

'Why shouldn't it?' Clare asked, trying not to remember all the bitter divorce cases she dealt with.

'Sometimes it seems impossible that I can feel this happy. Sometimes it worries me. And then I think, it's now that matters. Not tomorrow or the next day. But now. And that's what matters, isn't it, Clare? That we love each other now. We've got to make the most of it, haven't we? That's what life's all about. Now. Today.'

A tear fell onto the blue of the duvet, darkening it.

'Oh, don't take any notice of me, Clare. I'm just being silly and emotional. I bet John's not like this at all. Men aren't, are they? I expect he and Neal are having a good laugh about something at this very moment.'

She caught Clare's hand in hers and gazed pleadingly into her cousin's green eyes.

'You know all about marriage, don't you, Clare? It's part of your job — advising people — isn't it? Tell me I'm being silly. Tell me love does last.'

'Of course it does,' Clare answered, endeavouring to make her voice sound convincing, but still thinking of the sad people she saw every day of her life.

Had they rushed blindly into marriage, not caring, not even thinking? Or was Nicola different, filled with thistledown, floating high above the rest?

'Every bride has doubts, Nicky. It's quite natural. But there are only two people who can make your marriage work. No one else. Only you and John. Never forget that. Marriage is something you have to work at, not take for granted. Love each other, Nicky — whatever happens — love each other for always.' But in her own heart Clare doubted that her words were true.

'Come on, girls. Time's marching on and we mustn't keep that young man waiting, must we?'

Aunt Margaret was back, her face

carefully made up, her hair, loosened from its rollers, lying in rigid rows waiting to be brushed, her billowy body clad in a faded pink candlewick dressing-gown.

'The flowers have arrived and they're absolutely beautiful. Now tell me, Nicola, will my face do, or should I wear a little more mascara? I don't want it to run when I cry.'

The next hour passed in a whirl of activity. The bathroom wreathed in a mist of steam, scented with mingling fragrances; the button-holes and bouquets admired; dresses carefully lifted from their sheaths of polythene wrapping; hair-styles arranged and rearranged again; voices and excitement rising with every minute.

Nicola insisted on doing Clare's make-up. 'It's the one thing I am good at,' she said and smiled as Clare's green eyes grew softly muted beneath her expert fingers, her cheeks widened and glowed and her mouth bloomed into rosy softness; the sea-green silk dress making a perfect foil for the auburn of her thick, gently curving hair.

Finally they were both ready, standing there on the back lawn while Uncle Bill fetched his camera to take a few 'snaps' in the warm sunshine that had grown during the morning and now filled a clear, unclouded blue sky.

'We'd better be off, Clare,' advised Aunt Margaret, clutching at her hat as a tremor of wind dared to disturb it. 'The cars are here.'

Nicola stood, looking very young and vulnerable, then Uncle Bill slipped his arm round her waist and gave her a hug before stepping back, his eyes suddenly blurred, to take one last picture of 'my pretty little girl'.

Aunt Margaret dabbed at her cheek with a tiny scrap of lace. 'I've started weeping already and the service hasn't even begun yet,' she whispered apologetically as Clare adjusted her aunt's veiled hat when she bent to step into the car, catching it against the roof.

'The bride's mother is allowed a

couple of tears, but not any more,' she soothed, giving one plump hand a squeeze. 'And anyway, why else would you wear a veil?'

*   *   *

The organ quavered, then a high note pealed out and there was a whisper of movement while heads turned and hymn-sheets rustled open as everyone rose to their feet, and Uncle Bill proudly led his daughter down the aisle to a crescendo of triumphant music.

Clare followed, a mixture of emotions flooding through her at the solemnity of the occasion and the flower-filled beauty of the ancient church, its tall stone columns and white walls bright with sunshine.

Two grey-clad backs, stiff and upright, moved into position and when Nicola reached her bridegroom a look of such depth passed between them that it seared right through Clare. This was what love was all about. Never mind what happened in years to come. Never mind if heartbreak was to follow. They loved each other now. And now was what mattered. Happiness, however brief, was there for all to see.

★   ★   ★

'Am I allowed to take your arm?' Neal breathed in Clare's ear while they waited in the vestry for the register to be signed, ready to move back down the aisle. 'Or would that be quite against your rules?'

Even here, thought Clare, in the reverence of this beautiful church, he was mocking her.

'Of course you have to take my arm,' she retorted. 'It's the tradition. We all walk down the aisle in pairs. Bride and groom. Bridesmaid and best man. Mother of the bride and bridegroom's father. Mother of the groom and bride's father.'

Humour glinted in his dark eyes. 'I believe the bridesmaid is regarded as best man's perks for the day — all part of the tradition too, I hasten to add.'

His fingers took hers and drew her arm through his, holding it firmly there, when they followed behind the bridal pair to the thunder of the 'Wedding March' as it pealed up to the wood of the dark arched rafters, almost drowning the sound of the bells.

Sunbeams filtered through the scarlet and blue of the windows, patterning the stone pillars and walls with a tapestry of different hues, rivalling the blaze of colour from enormous bowls of flowers filling their sills.

On every side faces smiled their greeting and the whole church was filled with such gladness and contentment that Clare's throat ached. She was aware of a tightening of the fingers clasping hers and looked up into Neal's eyes to find the usual mockery gone and in its place a look so deep and unfathomable that it made a wave of intensity prickle down her spine.

Outside in the sunshine he left her

and she felt a sense of loss, watching him take charge, assisting the photographer, directing the various relations into correct family groupings; talking to those obviously on their own, soothing an aged great-aunt who had mislaid her gloves.

He did it all so easily, so calmly, so unobtrusively. Clare longed for someone to direct her own life like that, to tell her exactly when and how to do things; to smooth the path for her.

Nicola and John, lost in their own world, moved hand in hand together, their faces bright with faraway smiles while their eyes constantly turned to each other.

Seeing them, Clare felt desperately alone, knowing somehow that what she felt for Geoffrey was not love at all, not even attraction.

Once she had been flattered that he, one of the partners in the firm, should take such an interest. First in her work, then in herself as time progressed. On several occasions, when they'd had to work late, there'd been dinner together, somewhere quiet and secluded — where others wouldn't discover or even notice them.

His wife Eileen, he told her, was devoted to their two sons; a marvellous mother, but not, apparently, a marvellous wife. After coping with them, she was always too tired to go out with Geoffrey in the evenings, content to stay at home watching the latest soap opera on television.

But Geoffrey liked a social life, good food, good wine, good company. And he needed someone to share them with him.

Eileen, he said, spent so much time with the children, she even thought like one now; her conversation being only of them, what they did, what they said; who'd been for coffee or tea. What he needed, Geoffrey told her, was a woman with a brain, intelligence, vitality.

What he needed, he said, was Clare.

And so, at first, she was flattered. A

brilliant man like Geoffrey, highly thought of in the legal profession, erudite, wealthy and mature, actually wanting her.

Her future with the firm was assured, he said. A girl like her. A man like him. When the senior partner retired, he would take over, and then . . .

Clare was ambitious — and anxious to prove herself in a world full of successful men.

So what was love? It didn't last. She knew that only too well. As a child she'd seen her parents' love waver and finally die. Now, in her job, she saw it happening every day of her life.

And marriage? What was that? Just an image, a mirage that vanished.

Yet here she was, surrounded by an aura of love. It was everywhere. Families gathered together. Faces full of joy. Everyone happy and contented. Delighted as they gazed at the happy couple.

Thistledown. That was Nicola's description of love.

Was its future only to be scattered and gone for ever with one harsh breeze?

Is life making me cynical? Clare wondered. All I ever hear is the bitterness, the heartbreak, the hatred, the sorrow. All I ever see are the broken marriages, not the happy ones.

Not those like Aunt Margaret and Uncle Bill standing, hands entwined, after a lifetime together. I've forgotten what love means. Yet here it surrounds me — the love of families, the love of friends, of everyone.

'A penny for those thoughts.' Neal was beside her, a glass of champagne in either hand.

She smiled at him sadly. 'I doubt they're worth even a penny.'

'So sombre? Then you must be reviewing your life — and not liking it one bit,' he said, reading her mind yet again.

'How did you guess?' she replied, tasting the dry sharpness of the wine.

'With some people you know exactly

what they're thinking. I believe it's called affinity . . . or maybe love,' he added softly.

His face was close to hers and she could feel the warmth from his skin, see the fringe of his lashes thickly outlining those caring brown eyes, the hint of a shadow beginning to darken his chin.

Was it the wine that made her want to reach up and bring his mouth down to hers? Or just the hypnotic, romantic effect of such an occasion?

And would he, once again, read her thoughts?

As if in reply, his fingers were tilting her chin, holding it still as he kissed her, his lips moving softly over hers — and instantly the spell was broken. Quickly she pulled away, angry with herself for letting him take advantage of her vulnerability.

'What's wrong?'

Surprise flared into his eyes at her change of mood, then the mocking light was back again.

'Oh, I see. Maybe I should've let you

make the first move, is that it?'

He gave a short cynical laugh. 'I thought I'd detected a tiny chink in that armour, believing that once that business-like black suit and white blouse were removed, and the fairy princess revealed in such glorious splendour, all I had to do was awaken her with a kiss.'

To Clare's annoyance he still cupped her chin firmly in his hand — and yet somehow she was loath for him to remove it.

'Why do you hide behind that façade, Clare?' he asked gently. 'Why pretend you're a thick-skinned career-woman when it's blatantly obvious you're not? Just look at you.'

His dark eyes moved over her in a way that made her cheeks flame.

'Do you realise the effect you've created? Those delightful shoulders rising up from a sea of aquamarine like Aphrodite from the waves? That hair the colour of marigolds blazing on a summer day? That mouth that tries so hard to stay taut and yet so often reveals, with your eyes, every emotion you endeavour to conceal? Why, Clare?'

'Please let go of my chin.' Her green eyes glinted dangerously as she reached up to pull away his hand and found her own caught and held.

'Today,' he said, looking down at her without the slightest trace of apology, 'tradition declares you're mine whether you like it or not, so take that look of fury off your beautiful face and smile. We are about to sit down for the wedding feast and as you will be next to me, I don't want the cream on my trifle curdled before I can eat it.'

Slowly his fingers released her own and she lowered her hand feeling as if it were on fire.

'Relax, Clare. You're as taut as a violin string. Now smile sweetly for the photographers. We don't want to spoil the wedding-album for Nicky and John, do we?'

3

Everything was merging into a blur. A sea of faces gazing back at her; smiling; laughing; clapping as speeches were made, cards read out loud, toasts proclaimed.

Clare's head was beginning to ache with it all. She wanted to get away, anywhere. Away from the noise, the constant clatter of plates and glasses, the deafening chatter of voices, rising and falling; the heat. Everything.

And most of all she wanted to get away from the closeness of Neal, feeling the brush of his sleeve on her arm, seeing the movement of his head, the curve of his mouth, the expression in his eyes when he turned to her.

Why did weddings have this effect? This lulling of the senses. This heightening of awareness. Creating silly romantic fantasies.

★　★　★

The bride and groom were leaving now. Leaving in a swirl of confetti and enchantment. Nicky — her tawny upswept hair topped by a froth of pale-blue veiling and tiny forget-me-not flowers, her huge grey eyes misted by tears as she kissed everyone goodbye, her face almost ethereal in its beauty — was standing at the foot of the hotel steps, tossing her posy of rosebuds and lily of the valley high in the air.

Hands reached out eagerly to catch it — and Clare deliberately stood back, letting it fall to the ground at her feet.

Neal bent to pick it up and hand it to her.

'More tradition,' he smiled. 'Whoever catches the bouquet is the next to wed.'

'But nobody caught it,' replied Clare, looking sideways, not daring to meet his eyes and read the message in them.

'They were intended for you.'

He still held out the flowers, but Clare turned away, hating herself for doing so, wanting to take them and forget her stupid, stubborn pride.

Everyone was clustered round the bridal car, calling out last-minute messages, waving, blowing kisses as it slowly drove off. Clare tried to move away but was swept along with the guests when they went back into the hotel, everyone eager for the evening's entertainment.

A disco had been set up in the ballroom and was already filling the air with music. Clare wished she'd kept to her original intention of returning to London immediately after the ceremony. She was swamped by a confusion of emotions, feelings she wasn't prepared for; exhausted by the overwhelming effect of the day

What would happen if she stayed?

An arm closed lightly round her waist and, thinking it was Neal, she was about to pull away until she realised it was Uncle Bill, his face bleak with sadness.

'Will you do me the honour of the

first dance, Clare?' he asked, and seeing such desolation in his eyes, she couldn't refuse.

Poor Uncle Bill. Clare remembered him when she and Nicky were children, always there in the background. He never said much. Aunt Margaret was the positive one, but Uncle Bill had a quiet presence about him. A reliability.

He was the one who'd mend their broken dolls or toys without a fuss. Just silently getting on with the job, finding a tube of glue or his box of tools. There had always been a feeling of safety with Uncle Bill, knowing that whatever disaster happened, he would sort things out patiently without any fuss.

'I'll miss her,' he said quietly.

'But she's not going far, Uncle Bill. They'll still be living in the town,' Clare comforted him.

His lined face puckered into a smile. 'Could be worse, I suppose. But I'll still miss her. She always made my life — and this house — brim with joy, you know. Especially these last months. It's going to be so quiet.'

'Not with Aunt Margaret around,' Clare laughed, watching her aunt chattering away nineteen to the dozen in the middle of a group of people across the wide room.

'You will come back to see us, won't you, Clare?' His voice was gentle as he said it. 'Don't cut yourself off from everyone. It's nice for you to enjoy your job, but you still need people, you know. And with your mother in America now . . . Don't forget we're always here whenever you need us.'

'Thanks, Uncle Bill. I won't forget that.'

A lump was rising in her throat, threatening to choke her. Despite his own sadness, he was still concerned about her life too.

'He's a nice lad,' he said, after a pause.

'John, you mean?'

'No, I was talking about Neal. He's a nice lad.'

53

Uncle Bill's faded blue eyes studied her shrewdly.

'Not matchmaking, are you?' she smiled. 'One wedding in the family is quite enough.'

'You'd make a nice couple — and you've a lot in common.'

'With that arrogant man?' Clare's tone was scathing.

'Both being solicitors, I mean.'

Clare's green eyes widened. 'He's a *solicitor*?'

'Neal's father has a practice in the town. Didn't he tell you?'

'No, he did not,' Clare replied grimly.

After all he'd said on the train too. No wonder he didn't think much of women in the profession.

'Bill!'

Aunt Margaret was calling from the other side of the room.

'Mary and Jim are just leaving. Come and say goodbye, dear.'

With a murmur of apology he moved to join her and Clare was left in a corner, too far from the door to make her escape.

'What are you doing tomorrow?'

Her back stiffened. Neal's hand was there, firmly guiding her onto the dance-floor.

'Going back to London.'

Her steps began automatically to follow his.

'What time?'

'I haven't decided yet. Early if I can.'

'Must you? Surely there's no rush? I want to take you over to Minsmere. You'd like that.'

'Minsmere?'

'It's a stretch of coast and marshland that's been turned into a nature reserve. Very peaceful. It'll do you good to unwind. I'll be round to collect you about ten. We'll have lunch somewhere and you can catch the evening train.'

Clare hesitated, then shook her head. 'No. I must get back to London. I've heaps to do.'

'For instance?'

She hated his persistence.

'Being a solicitor, you should know,' she retorted.

He pursed his lips in a wry grimace, raising his eyebrows in mock alarm.

'Ah. You've discovered my guilty secret then?'

'No wonder you're so biased against women working in the same profession.'

'Not at all. As I told you before, I think they can be very good, but they can get emotionally involved and that to my mind is bad, both for them and their clients.'

'I'm too tired to go into all that argument again,' Clare protested wearily. 'Just take it I don't agree though.'

His dark eyes were full of concern. 'I'm sorry. It's been a long day and it is getting late. Would you like me to take you back to Bill and Margaret's cottage?'

'We can't very well leave, can we?'

'Who's to know?'

A smile filled her eyes as she looked back at him. 'Well, the best man and bridesmaid are rather conspicuous, you know. And you are supposed to be in charge of the whole do this evening, aren't you?'

He nodded ruefully. 'I suppose you're right. It might be difficult. How about if I make sure the DJ only plays soft soothing music that we can drift to for the rest of the night? How would that suit you?'

'I'd probably nod off,' she laughed.

'Well, provided it's on my shoulder, I shan't complain,' he said lightly.

In the tiny crowded space left for dancing, there was little room to do more than sway together in time to the music and Clare let herself drift in Neal's arms, quite content to be there, his cheek resting against her hair.

There was one question that had been puzzling her all day. She had to know the answer.

He was a very attractive man. Surely there must be someone . . . and yet he was here alone.

'Why aren't you married, Neal?'

For a moment his body stiffened and

his face tensed, a pulse flickering rapidly in his cheek.

'I was,' he replied quietly, 'but not any more.'

Before she could ask why, the music ended and Aunt Margaret was beckoning her over to meet a collection of neighbours and friends who remembered her as a little girl.

By the time they'd recounted various incidents in her childhood and she'd managed to identify everyone, another hour had gone, but all the while she was aware of Neal dutifully carrying out his role as best man and dancing with almost every lady in the room.

'What about tomorrow?' he asked, catching her arm as Aunt Margaret and Uncle Bill hustled her out of the door at the end of the evening. 'Will you let me take you over to Minsmere?'

'I'm sorry, but I must get back to London, Neal.'

'Then I'll drive you to the station.'

*   *   *

The cottage had an uneasy air about it next morning. Even Aunt Margaret was quiet and Clare found her in Nicola's room, sitting on the bed, holding the crumpled wedding-dress in her arms, with a lost look on her plump round face.

'Promise you'll come back and see us, Clare,' she begged. 'I wish you'd stay on a little longer. It would do you good. Must you leave so soon?'

'I'm sorry, Aunt Margaret, but I really do have a great deal of work to get through. We've several important cases coming up soon and I've a lot to prepare for them.'

'Let's make a definite date before you go then.'

Her aunt's eyes suddenly brimmed with tears. 'We want to have something to look forward to now that all the excitement's over.'

'Oh, Aunt Margaret,' Clare cried, putting her arm round the quivering shoulders and hugging her. 'Of course I'll come.'

At that moment Neal arrived to drive her to the station and carried her bag out to the car while she said goodbye, leaving her aunt and uncle standing forlornly by the gate like two lost souls.

Dismay filled her when she saw his car.

'Somehow, I thought a man in your exalted position would drive an expensive BMW or Rover, not an old banger,' she confessed, staring at the low-slung red-painted ancient sports model parked by the edge of the green.

'That kind of thing is extremely pretentious and merely a status symbol,' Neal informed her sternly, dumping her case in the back.

'I should've guessed you'd think like that,' Clare observed, hitching up her straight black skirt to swing her legs into the confined space under the dashboard.

His dark eyes followed the movement with obvious approval and she felt her face flush slightly. 'I only hope it doesn't rain.'

Already the sky was looking ominous, with heavy banks of cloud piling up over the sea and moving in swiftly.

'Where are we going?' she questioned after a mile or so as Neal swung the car off the main road, along a lane. 'This isn't the way to the station.'

'No, it's the way to Minsmere. I said I wanted to take you there.'

'But I don't want to go. I told you that, Neal, quite positively, yesterday,' she protested. 'And anyway, my train leaves in half an hour.'

'There'll be another,' he replied placidly, changing gear.

The car gathered speed, the flat open countryside racing past, the wind lifting her hair and swirling it round her face in wraith-like strands, then they were bumping along a deeply-rutted track.

'You are the most insufferable man I've ever met! Don't you take any notice of what people say?' she fumed. 'I told you I must get back to London. I've half a dozen cases to attend to. I need to get down to some work.'

61

'And remember what your aunt said — you'll do it far better after a rest. Just relax, Clare. You really should untense a little. One of these days you're going to crack.'

He was driving over gravel now, easing the car into a parking position beneath a sandy cleft in the hillside, where sand martins dipped and swooped in and out of tiny nest-holes.

'Right then,' he said, leaning back and squinting up at the sky which was growing more threatening with every minute. 'What have you brought to put on your feet?'

'I didn't exactly come prepared for monsoons or marshes,' Clare retorted drily. 'I am wearing my one and only pair of black suede high heels. Somehow I doubt they'll be suitable for whatever you have in mind, so shall we go back to the station now?'

'Not to worry.' He grinned. 'There's a spare pair of wellies in the back and you can borrow my cagoule. That stylish suit may look good for the judge but I doubt the wildfowl will appreciate it soaking wet.'

'Look, Neal. I don't want either your wellies or your cagoule. Just drive me back to the station while there's still time.'

He glanced at his watch. 'Too late I'm afraid, and there won't be another train until after lunch. Come on, you might as well enjoy it while you're here, Clare.'

'I shan't, and your boots will be far too big anyway.'

With a grin he produced a couple of pairs of thick knitted socks from the pocket of his jacket and kneeling down on the gravel began to remove her shoes.

'I can do that,' she said swiftly, lifting her legs away, and began to roll on the socks, then slid her feet into the long green boots.

The jacket came down almost to her knees and muffled her neck, but there was a faint smell of aftershave on the collar which gave it a comforting feel that she had to admit to herself she enjoyed.

As the first odd spots of rain began to fall, Neal snapped the hood of the sports car into place and, gripping her elbow firmly, hurried her along a well-trodden path to the nearest hide, a small wooden hut overlooking one of the smaller lakes.

Their feet clumped on the bare planks of the floor and a smell of creosote and warm wood met them as they settled onto the narrow bench in front of the slit-like windows.

'If you're lucky we'll see an avocet,' Neal whispered, his mouth brushing her ear as he spoke, and for a fleeting moment she wanted to turn her head to meet his lips.

There was an empty silence hanging over the water, its surface barely ruffled by the slight wind that preceded the rain. Reeds stood straight and spear-like, quivering. Glistening patches of mud were etched with a tracing of delicate footprints. A coot stalked from the shelter of some tall grasses, dipping its beak. Across the sky a flight of mallards wheeled before skidding to rest, feet first, ending in a trail of rising spray.

'We might make it to the next hide down by the sea before the storm comes.'

Neal took her hand and led her along a grassy path between high beds of reeds that rustled eerily in the rising wind as they stretched thickly away on either side.

When they reached the shore the full force of the east wind met them, biting sharply into their cheeks, making Clare sway for a second before they turned to crunch over pebbles until they came to the next hide, looking across the wetlands, and climbed its steep steps.

A violent flash of lightning split the sky and at the same time a crack of thunder echoed, trembling the wood beneath their feet. Clare shuddered, staring up with frightened eyes at the darkness that was rapidly closing in, her fingers clutching the sleeve of Neal's tweed jacket.

He tugged open the door of the hide and pushed her inside, as it was caught by a gust of wind, slamming it behind them. Neal leaned against the ledge of the long, low window, watching with fascination as the sky was split in all directions by brilliant jags of light.

Like a torrent the rain began, sheeting down, veiling the lake. Water dripped through one corner of the roof, slowly gathering into a steady stream that ran across the floor like a tiny river, surrounding their feet.

Clare felt they were the only people left in a world of desolation as she saw the reeds bordering the lakes flatten until they touched the water, its surface dimpled by ever-widening circles when the rain came in flurries.

'Why on earth did you bring me here?' she wailed, shaking with fear as another crash of thunder shook the whole structure of the fragile building.

'Because it's just the place to be in a

storm. It's magnificent, Clare. Look. There's a whole vista out there. That vast expanse of open sky. The dramatic effect on the lakes. It really is quite fantastic, even you must agree.'

He touched her rain-wet cheek with a gentle finger. 'There's no need to be frightened. It's only a thunderstorm, Clare.'

'And what if this thing gets struck by lightning?' she managed to protest in a trembling voice. 'We'll both go up in smoke.'

His tanned face broke into a teasing grin. 'What better place to die, with me to hold your hand. Don't worry though. It's not very likely with all this space around.'

'Of course it is. It's just the sort of place to be struck. A solitary hut in the middle of nowhere. The one and only ideal spot.'

'Do you always need to be right, Clare? Is that part of your success in court? You have to win?' he said regretfully.

In the distance a faint silvering of brightness appeared over the trees and the force of the rain eased to a steady downpour. The lakes were quite deserted now and Clare wondered where all the waterfowl were hiding. She hadn't noticed them disappear.

'Don't go back to London, Clare. Stay here.' Neal's voice was strangely uneven, his dark eyes pleading.

'In these bleak and desolate marshes?' she enquired.

'It's not always like this. There's a peace and tranquillity about the place. Surely you've noticed that? No hustle and bustle. No rush and frenetic chasing here and there. No pressures.'

He reached out to take her hand. 'Stay here. Please, Clare.'

'And what about my job?'

'Is it so important?'

'Of course it is.'

'Then join our practice. My father will be retiring in a year or so. We shall need another good brain to bridge the gap.'

He smiled down at her. 'It may not have all the excitement you find in London. There'd be the odd parking fine, maybe a spot of conveyancing, or dispute over land. The occasional divorce. Nothing dramatic or scandalous though. Old ladies don't get mugged around here, or young ones raped and murdered for that matter. It's very quiet, but pleasant all the same. I'm sure you'd grow to like it — and I know I would.'

'You're offering me a job?'

'I'm offering you more than a job, Clare. I want to marry you.'

'Marry me!' Her voice rose on a high note.

'Is that so far-fetched? I'm a man of decision. No beating about the bush. And I want to marry you, Clare.'

He turned her face to his. 'Am I so very repulsive?'

Her body was trembling now, but not from the storm. She should be filled with anger, but it wasn't that either.

This man whom she'd only met the previous day, who'd told her in no uncertain manner exactly what he thought of women who tried to do his job, who'd taken not the slightest notice of what she thought or wanted to do — this man was actually asking her to marry him. How audacious could he get?

'You can only be joking,' she said quietly.

'How can I prove to you I'm not?'

His mouth was moving closer as he spoke, his wet hair brushing her forehead, then their lips touched and he pulled her against him with a sudden roughness that surprised and excited her.

For a second she held back, but the force of his mouth on hers was too strong and she responded in a way she couldn't prevent.

'Now do you believe me?' he asked huskily.

A shaft of sunlight splintered through the raindrops on the glass of the window, making a rainbow of brightness across her face, dazzling her eyes as she looked up at him, filled with a bewildering confusion of emotions.

The storm had gone. Already the smoothness of the lake had returned, clusters of wildfowl appearing on its surface, bobbing and darting, heads down, tails up.

An elegant, slender black and white bird stood on delicate spindle legs, its upward-curved beak poised.

Neal caught her arm.

'An avocet,' he breathed and as they watched a second bird appeared close beside it. 'You're lucky to see one, let alone a pair.'

His hand held hers as they walked back to the car along the rain-drenched paths, and then he turned to ask again, 'Will you marry me?'

Resolutely Clare shook her head.

'But why?'

'I can't.'

'There's someone else?' His face suddenly darkened. 'Or is it that wretched career?'

She felt a prickle of anger at his tone. Why did it always come back to her job? Why couldn't he accept that she, as much as he, wanted to be successful in what she did?

'No, not only that,' she said, 'but divorce is the one aspect of law I specialise in, so I know only too well that marriage usually ends in heartbreak. Surely you must know that, even if you do live in such peaceful seclusion. You only have to read the newspaper any day. What are the statistics? One in three marriages fails? You've been married, haven't you? You should know the facts.'

She saw an expression of pain fill his eyes and knew she'd touched on a raw spot.

'What time's my train?' she asked, wanting to change the subject.

He pushed back the sleeve of his jacket and glanced at his watch.

'Just over an hour,' he answered bleakly. 'We'll stop to eat on the way.'

* * *

At the station he made one last plea.
'I don't want to lose you, Clare.'

* * *

As she sat back in the corner of the
carriage, she took the notes of Miss
Milsom's will from her bag and began
to read, biting back the rush of tears
that threatened to overwhelm her.

4

Clare had hardly arrived back in her London flat when the telephone rang. For a second her heart missed a beat. Was Neal really so persistent?

Trying to breathe slowly, she picked up the receiver and gave her name, eager to hear his voice again.

'Clare.'

Disappointment surged through her. It was Geoffrey.

'Thank goodness you're back. Look, there's a lad who's coming in for an interview tomorrow morning. Ed Booker. He's in court in the afternoon. Can you do it for me? It'll mean going in to the office now to pick up the file. You'll need to read up on the case this evening.'

'But Geoffrey, I've only just got home. I haven't even had a chance to unpack yet, or have a cup of coffee.'

'It's urgent, Clare. I shan't be in tomorrow until heaven knows when. One of the boys has broken his arm. He has to go back to the hospital for more X-rays.'

'Can't Eileen take him?' Clare protested.

'Eileen? Of course not. She can't bear anything like that. No, Clare. I must take Jonathan. He wants me with him anyway.'

'But you've been dealing with the Booker case for weeks now, Geoffrey. It's that vicious knifing, isn't it?'

'That's right. Poor little blighter. Anyway, all the details are in the file. If you have any problems, just give me a ring.'

His voice went suddenly low. 'And Clare, don't forget I love you.'

Was that the little extra sweetener to persuade her to do what he wanted? Clare wondered cynically.

Reluctantly she put on her jacket again and caught a taxi across London, entering the glass-fronted building and climbing the stairs to the third floor where their offices were situated. Being Sunday the lifts weren't working and no one was around.

Clare felt as if eyes were watching her when she crossed the landing and unlocked the main door. It gave her a creepy feeling. Just suppose someone was lurking?

It was a thought that often worried her. They had several unpleasant characters as clients and she often wondered just how some of them might react if you met them in a dark alley, after their case had gone the wrong way.

Her footsteps echoed on the highly-polished floor when she walked through the corridors until she reached Geoffrey's office and opened his door.

Someone gripped her arm and she let out a shriek of terror, almost fainting with shock as she did so.

'Ssh! It's only me.'

Geoffrey's mouth slid warmly down the back of her neck as he buried his face in her hair.

'What on earth are you doing here?' she gasped. 'You frightened me to death.'

'It was the only way I could think of for seeing you again. I missed you, darling.'

'But I thought you couldn't get away from home? That was why you sent me to get your wretched file.'

'Just as excuse, darling. I couldn't tell Eileen I was burning with desire to see you, could I? She came into the room when I started making the phone call and it was the only way I could think of to meet you here — alone.'

His fingers were on the collar of her blouse, reaching for the buttons. Clare pushed them away.

'What's the matter? Why the reluctance? We've got the whole place to ourselves, darling.'

'Just give me the file, Geoffrey. Or was that an excuse too? I've got a taxi waiting.'

'Of course I want you to conduct the case for me. I told you I probably shan't be in tomorrow. But Clare, this isn't like you, darling. What's up?'

'I've just travelled all the way back from Suffolk, Geoffrey. I'm exhausted. It's been a hectic couple of days. All I want now is to get some sleep. Anyway, I thought Eileen and your son were both too distraught to be left without you.'

'There's no need for sarcasm,' he said tersely. 'It doesn't suit you. Has this wedding put your nose out of joint or something? Turned you broody? Be patient, darling. It'll be your turn one day, but until then let's make the most of what time we've got.'

His hand slid down her back, drawing her towards him, his lips crushing down hard onto hers — and suddenly she could remember again the warm smell of creosoted wood and the dampness of a tweed jacket . . .

Twisting her face away from Geoffrey's, she looked into his pale eyes, seeing the puzzled anger that filled them.

'My taxi's waiting,' she said, opening the cabinet drawer and selecting a file.

'I'll be waiting for you tomorrow, Clare.'

Turning quickly, she hurried back to the landing and ran down the stairs.

What's happening to me? she thought desperately. Only days ago I'd have welcomed an opportunity to be alone with Geoffrey, but now . . .

As the taxi passed an untidy overgrown stretch of wasteland on the outskirts of the town, a drift of thistledown floated in the air and she watched it rise high into the blue of the sky, her throat aching with sadness.

⋆ ⋆ ⋆

It was a difficult case. Young Booker had been caught with a group of toughs, all running away from where another youth lay bleeding on the pavement, stabbed several times in the stomach.

Booker insisted he had merely been

79

walking along the street, when the others rushed past him, chased by the police, and he'd been swept along with them, then — unfairly — arrested.

It could easily be true, Clare thought. If only Ed Booker didn't look such a villain. Just seeing him sitting there in front of her, with his cropped bullet-head and pig-like eyes, that twisted mess of a nose, those lurid tattoos patterning his forehead and each cheek and covering his thick muscular arms, Clare knew any court would instantly condemn him, however innocent he might be.

'Now look, Ed. You were involved, weren't you?'

She tried to meet his narrow eyes as she went on: 'Do you possess a weapon?'

The youth stared at her blankly. 'Eh?'

'Have you got a knife, Ed?'

He leaned forward, undoing one of the many zips on his leather jacket, and thrust a thin-bladed weapon viciously into the polished wood of her desk, half-grinning as she jerked backwards in alarm.

'Only that one?' she asked in a steady voice.

'Have now,' he muttered, moving a wad of gum to the other side of his mouth to speak.

'But you did have another knife?'

'Not any more, gorgeous.' The tattooed skull on his pale forehead creased as he smiled at her.

'What happened to your other knife, Ed?' she said patiently.

'Lost it, didn't I?'

'When?'

'Dunno.'

'Look, Ed. It's important. You'll be asked in court this afternoon if the weapon that stabbed that boy belonged to you. Did it?'

The pig-like eyes crinkled. 'I wouldn't say if it did, would I? I'm not stupid, am I?'

'If you did stab him, it would be better if you told me so now and stopped wasting my time, Ed. If they prove you guilty, you'll get a much stiffer sentence than if you admitted your guilt, you know.'

'Last time they took me in,' he said, moving the gum to the other cheek and testing it with his tongue as it passed. 'Last time, I did community service. Cushy number that was. Planting trees. Six weeks out in the sunshine. Middle of June I started. Got a smashing tan. Better than the Coster Braver, that was.'

'Well this time it'll probably be prison,' Clare retorted grimly.

'Inside?'

The jaws stopped chewing.

'Me dad's inside. Might meet him then, mightn't I?'

'Look, Ed. I want the truth. Were you with that group of yobs or not? One of them's sure to split if you were?'

A slow smile widened his mouth and he ran one finger thoughtfully down the blade of the knife quivering in the desk top.

'Nah,' he said. 'None of them'll split,

not on me they won't. Anyway, you're going to get me off. Pretty lady like you, must have all them blokes in that court waiting to get right up your skirt. Nah, I'll get off. You'll see to that, won't you, gorgeous.'

There was no mistaking the threat in his voice, his lips still smiling a smile that didn't reach the tiny eyes staring into her face.

This was a part of the job Clare hated, dealing with the bully-boys, the future hardened criminals, knowing that whatever she did or said, nothing would change the path laid out for them.

Could a youth like Ed have been something different or was his destiny planned from the very second of his creation? Some of the kids she met she felt didn't have a chance, but this one was evil. Every instinct in her said he was guilty and yet, knowing that, she had to stand up in court and defend him, because he would never admit otherwise.

And that really sickened her.

★　★　★

After he'd gone, the stale smell of his clothes still hung in the air and she opened a window, breathing in the traffic-fumes as a slight relief.

Gazing out at the blue sky, she recalled that this time yesterday she'd been in Neal's little sports car, racing down narrow, winding leafy lanes, feeling the wind lift her hair, seeing out of the corner of her eye that handsome profile, the teasing smile that hovered round his lips.

But that was yesterday.

Abruptly she turned away and buzzed through for her next client.

The teenage girl who came in half-carrying a wriggling two-year-old looked hardly old enough to be out of school, let alone a mother. Jamie was a lively little scrap from his appearance, already running round the room, impatient to be gone again. Was he accident-prone, or was this quiet, shy girl a baby-batterer?

Clare looked at the dark bruises on the child's face. They could happen so easily. A polished floor. Toys scattered. Children fall.

Even now he was clambering up the handles of her filing-cabinet drawers. One slip and yet another bruise would show.

'They're going to take him away, miss. Don't let them.'

Tears were running down the girl's thin face, and she wiped at them with a shaking hand. 'He's just hyperactive, miss. That's what it is. I wouldn't hit him. Truly.'

Seeing the tears, the little boy ran over to his mother and climbed onto her lap, his small hands rubbing at her cheeks, his big eyes anxious as he covered her face with kisses.

Would a beaten child do that? Clare wondered.

And yet he had to be protected. It was up to her to discover whether Tracy was violent, or not. And appearances could be deceptive.

One more client to fit in before lunch. Clare checked her diary. Oh no, not Mrs Poulton. No wonder her husband had walked out. Living with such a bitter and spiteful woman, it was surprising he'd stayed so long. And now she was vindictive too. That man was going to suffer if his wife had her way.

Why was it that she so often felt on the side of the opposing party, Clare wondered, seeing exactly why they acted as they had? It would be so much easier, sometimes, to swap clients and act for the other side.

'No way is that bitch going to have my house,' Mrs Poulton raged, sitting there in a fur coat despite the warmth of the day, her blonded hair elegantly curled into a youthful style, her face thick with make-up and mascara. An overpowering smell of Chanel No. 5 mixed with nervous perspiration made Clare wish she'd left the window open.

'First she takes my husband, now she

wants my home as well. She's destroyed my marriage, that woman has.'

'That's not quite true, Mrs Poulton,' Clare reminded her. 'Your husband never met the co-respondent until nearly a year after he left you.'

'So he says,' scorned Mrs Poulton.

'She only moved down from Scotland six months ago, Mrs Poulton,' Clare pointed out.

'And acted fast. First man she could lay her hands on, I don't doubt. Mervin always was a soft touch. Any sob-story would take him in. That's why we never had a penny.'

'You have no children, Mrs Poulton. There's no reason why you can't take a job.'

'Work? Me? When I've a husband to provide for me? Slaved my fingers to the bone, I have, over the years. Turned that little house into a palace, I have. And what happens? He walks out on me. Just like that. No warning. And for what reason may I ask?'

'Don't you think your husband may

have grown a little tired of always being the one to provide? You do have rather lavish tastes, don't you, Mrs Poulton? Holidays abroad twice a year. A dishwasher. Microwave. Automatic washing-machine. Are all those really necessary if you're on such a limited income?'

'It's my right, isn't it? What a husband *should* provide. Why else would I marry him?'

'I'm afraid in this day and age it's a case of equal rights, Mrs Poulton. Most women prefer to share, both work and leisure. What were you trained to do? You worked before your marriage, didn't you?'

The woman sitting in front of her glared. 'Does it matter? I've been married for over seven years now. This is my life, not what I did before. I expect to be kept in the way to which I've become accustomed. He married me, didn't he?'

'Yes, Mrs Poulton, but people change over the years — especially if they don't try to pull together. There must have been some reason for your husband to leave you.'

'There was,' she snorted. 'That woman!'

'But not at first, Mrs Poulton,' Clare repeated, flicking back through her file of papers. 'It was several months before your husband even met her, as I mentioned before. He'd already left you then. Why?'

'Why? Ask him that, not me. How should I know?'

'You must have some idea. Did you have arguments? You admit you had money problems. What about your sex life?'

An angry flush darkened the woman's skin. 'There's no need to go into all that,' she replied stiffly.

'I think there is, Mrs Poulton. From your husband's petition, it appears to be a very definite reason.'

Mrs Poulton moved awkwardly on her chair, then leaned forward confidentially.

'If you must know, my husband's

over-sexed. Quite obsessed with it.'

'I see.' Clare found it difficult to keep a straight face as she looked at the woman.

'I'd rather not go into details, if you don't mind. I found it all very distressing at the time.'

'It says in his petition that you hadn't slept together for more than six years.'

'Well that's a lie for a start,' Mrs Poulton protested indignantly. 'Mervin only moved into the spare room a couple of years ago.'

'So you still had a sexual relationship until about two years ago.' Clare made a note on the file.

Mrs Poulton looked uncomfortable. 'Do you mean . . . '

'Did you or did you not have sex with your husband?' Clare asked impatiently. Why beat around the bush any longer? The woman must know what she meant.

'No.'

'So your husband's statement is true?'

'If that's what you mean, then yes it is.'

Clare sighed. It was going to be a long day.

★　★　★

Most of the afternoon was spent in court with Ed Booker. As she expected, he received a prison sentence. At least, she thought, they'd be spared seeing him for a while, although she had no doubt he'd be back in court on yet another charge soon after he was released again. Youths like Ed Booker always were. They knew no other way of life.

Geoffrey was waiting for her in the corridor when she came out of her office at five o'clock.

'How's Jonathan's arm?' she felt obliged to ask.

'Oh, coming along nicely,' he replied, his fingers cool on her wrist, lightly caressing the smooth skin.

'Look, Clare, I must talk to you. Can

we find somewhere for a drink?'

She glanced at her watch.

'Just fifteen minutes then. I must rush home.'

At the back of her mind lingered the hope that Neal might phone.

Two of the secretaries walked past, chatting their way down the corridor. Geoffrey immediately began to ask about the Booker boy in a loud voice so that there could be no mistaking why he was talking to her.

'Guilty,' Clare said. 'There was no question about that, was there? We were only in court for half an hour, after spending ages waiting. He was sentenced to two years.'

'Two years! What was his reaction to that?'

'Bitter fury. What else can you expect from that kind of creature? He was taken down cursing women solicitors in general and me in particular. Somehow I don't think he has a very high opinion of us.'

Clare gave a wry smile, remembering

the threats Ed had made in her direction, his pig-like eyes full of hatred. 'He's a very nasty individual.'

'Maybe he'll have forgotten who you were by the time he comes out.'

'Somehow I doubt it.' She gave a slight shudder. 'Anyway, what did you want to see me about?'

'I'll tell you later, darling, not here.'

Geoffrey was steering her down the back stairs and out into the underground car-park. Carefully he unlocked his car door, brushing a speck of dust from the gleaming wing of the Rover as he did so.

'Let's try the wine bar in Tower Grove.'

'Won't Eileen be wondering where you are?' Clare couldn't resist the barbed question.

Geoffrey smiled. 'I told her I'd have to work late, having taken most of the day off to go to the hospital with Jonathan.'

'Well, I don't want to be too long. I've stacks to do. That wretched

Poulton case comes up at the end of the week.'

'The divorce?'

Clare nodded. 'I really can't stand the woman. She's like a leech, clinging onto that poor man. Why on earth she doesn't find a job and forget about him, I'll never know. She's quite venomous, determined to get every penny out of him that she can and ruin any hope of a future for him.'

'Probably can't bear the thought of rejection,' Geoffrey said, guiding the car skilfully through the gates of an old thatched building set among tall trees. 'It affects some women like that.'

The wine bar was crowded but eventually they found a secluded corner and Clare sat down.

'Now then, tell me why all the secrecy, Geoffrey?'

'It's about a trip away together, darling,' he replied, putting two brimming glasses of white wine down on the table.

Clare looked startled.

His hand closed over hers, smoothing the skin of her wrist with his fingers as he smiled at her.

'Trip?' she queried.

'I've been planning it for a couple of weeks now. I wasn't going to mention it until everything was finalised — and now it is.'

His heavy-lidded eyes glowed with satisfaction.

'I've discovered a quiet little hotel in Suffolk. It's miles away from anywhere. Just the place for a romantic idyll.'

5

'Suffolk?'

Clare stared back at him in growing dismay.

'It's booked for the end of the month. There's a conference being held near Southwold. Three days, mid-week, which is highly convenient as the boys won't have broken up by then, so Eileen will be fully occupied and won't be able to go with me. I shall tell her it's vital I attend, of course. She's used to me being away quite often nowadays.'

A doubtful look came into his eyes. 'The difficulty is that it's going to be rather noticeable if you and I are away at the same time. Of course, I could say it's an essential part of your legal training. It's either that, or pretending you're sick. That might be easier.'

'I can't do that,' Clare protested.

'Suppose someone called round to see how I am?'

'No trouble. You could say you have summer flu. Maybe take the Friday off as well, so that you're at your worst over the weekend. Then a few days away to recuperate. There is a bug going round at the moment, you know.'

'I can't lie, Geoffrey.'

'Of course you can! Really, Clare, you're far too sensitive. You need to develop a thicker skin. You'll never make a good solicitor unless you can lie convincingly.'

'That seems to be rather a strange statement to make.'

'But unfortunately it's true. You know and I know that some of our clients are probably as guilty as hell, but no way would they admit it, so we still have to stand up in court and plead their innocence. The better we do it, the more clients we attract. More wine, darling?'

'No, thanks. So what are you going to do? Do I accompany you officially as a member of the firm, or what?'

'Oh, I think I can fix it that you come officially, if that's what you prefer. Unfortunately there's sure to be someone we know, so it would soon get out you were with me, if I didn't.'

He raised his glass to his lips, savouring the golden liquid. 'It's conveyancing, something you may well decide to specialise in at a later date, if you really find litigation so traumatic. At least with house sales and purchases, you wouldn't get so easily upset at times.'

'I'm sorry, Geoffrey. I can't help it if some of the cases get to me. It's just that . . . '

Clare paused, recalling Neal's words on the train, and realised he was right after all.

'I find myself relating to some of the people.'

'You're far too sensitive, Clare darling, but I wouldn't have you any other way. Are you sure you won't have another glass of wine?'

'No, I really must get back.'

'Don't work too hard then. I want you fresh and relaxed when we go away together.'

'How can I be, when all you seem to do is pile your most unpleasant cases onto me?' Clare reminded him.

'Darling!'

'Well, it's true. I could do without the Ed Bookers and Mrs Poultons of this world, you know.'

'I'll call you a taxi, darling,' Geoffrey said smoothly, rising to his feet.

★   ★   ★

The telephone was ringing when she ran up the stairs and opened the flat door, but as she reached it the sound ceased.

Was it Neal?

Why did it matter so much? Why did she care?

Geoffrey had planned a trip away for them both, something she'd always wanted. So why, suddenly, did it no

99

longer have any appeal? And why, when Geoffrey's fingers were warm on her skin, did she remember the touch of other, more gentle hands?

She stood there, waiting, compelling it to ring again, but the phone was silent.

Then it occurred to her, how could Neal know her number or where she lived? She hadn't told him. He hadn't asked. Why should she expect him to ring at all?

The strident shrill note made her jump and her hand snatched the receiver from its rest, her heart pounding.

'Hullo.' Her voice was scarcely a whisper.

'Clare?' Eileen's soft tones reached her.

'Yes, Eileen.' Disappointment was surging through her body.

'Was Geoffrey in the office when you left? He warned me he'd be late, but when I phoned him there, I got no reply.'

There was a pause and Clare could hear Eileen take a deep breath.

'I thought you would be sure to know.'

What should she say?

If she told Eileen that Geoffrey was still there when she went home, and he told her a different story, what then?

'I did speak to him in the corridor before I went, Eileen.'

Well, that was the truth anyway.

'He said something about working late. I'm sure he must be on his way. Maybe the traffic's held him up?'

'Yes . . . maybe it has.'

'Did you call me earlier? About five minutes ago? Only the phone was ringing as I came in the door,' Clare asked hopefully.

'No,' came the reply. 'Oh, it's all right, Clare. I can hear Geoffrey's car. Sorry to have bothered you.'

★ ★ ★

She was eating her tea — a crispbread and cheese with a mug of strong black

101

coffee — when the phone rang again.

'At last! Presumably you were working late?'

For a second, Clare couldn't answer, listening to that voice again. Somehow it sounded deeper. Warmer, too. Phones have that effect.

'No. Not exactly.'

'Ah. An illicit meeting with your lover, no doubt.'

She knew he was teasing her. He couldn't know otherwise.

'Of course,' she replied lightly.

'Have you changed your mind yet?'

'About what?'

'Marrying me. I was being perfectly serious, you know.'

'Were you?' For a moment there was almost a wistful note in her voice, then it was gone. 'You know my views on marriage, Neal. It's a waste of time even to bother with it.'

'Surely you're not suggesting we live in sin then?'

The mocking tone was back again, all seriousness gone.

As if guessing her answer, he went on quickly: 'Look, Clare, I'm coming down to London shortly. A divorce case. May I see you? Perhaps in person, I can exert greater powers of persuasion.'

'Perhaps,' she said softly. 'When are you coming?'

'End of the month.'

'But . . .'

'No buts, Clare,' he said firmly. 'I'll see you then.'

She heard the faint click as the receiver was replaced and stood there, still clutching the phone in her hand as if willing him to continue the conversation.

The end of the month. That was when Geoffrey was taking her to Suffolk.

Why am I getting so paranoid about it? she thought. I don't even like the man. He's an arrogant chauvinist, determined to put down any woman who tries to equal him. What does it matter that he's coming to London? What does it matter that I won't be around to see him? I don't even *want* to see him.

'I don't,' she said out loud, as if trying desperately to convince herself.

★ ★ ★

Tracy Francis, the thin waif-like mother of Jamie, was waiting when she reached the office next morning, perched on the edge of one of the reception armchairs, her eyes red and swollen in a tragically white face.

'What's the matter, Tracy?' Clare asked, ushering the girl inside and requesting two cups of coffee from her secretary.

'They've took him, miss. Last night. Just come and took him.'

Tears were coursing down her cheeks and her bony little shoulders shook beneath the thin blue cotton of her tee-shirt as she tried unsuccessfully to wipe them away with the back of her hand.

'Who, Tracy? The Social Services?'

'I dunno, miss. A lady come . . . and a man. Said they had an order or something.' Her mouth quivered and the words were difficult to hear as she went on: 'They wouldn't even let me go with him, miss . . . He was screaming too. Clinging to me like he was stuck there with glue.'

Her eyes stared at Clare like violets drenched in rain. 'I never hurt him, miss. Truly I didn't.'

'It's all right, Tracy. Drink your coffee, while I make a couple of phone calls.'

Clare went out into the other office and used her secretary's phone, not wanting to upset Tracy any more, but there was nothing she could do. Jamie had been taken into care while enquiries were made as to the cause of his injuries.

What she did learn was that several old fractures had been discovered as well as recent damage to his left arm and shoulder.

'Probably caused by twisting or

pulling the child's limbs viciously,' a bland, expressionless voice informed her.

'Look, Tracy,' Clare said, going back into the room. 'I'll do everything I can, but at the moment that's not much, I'm afraid.'

She studied the girl carefully, trying to assess whether such a fragile-looking child would be capable of violence.

'Is Jamie very naughty?'

The tear-wet eyes stared back at her. 'Naughty? All kids are naughty, aren't they? Jamie's no worse than the rest.'

'Now I want you to be absolutely honest with me, Tracy. Do you smack him?'

The girl lowered her head.

'Sometimes,' she admitted.

'Look at me, Tracy. Do you smack him hard?'

An expression of pain filled the pathetic little face. 'No, miss. I'd never do that, but he does need a whack sometimes . . . when he really gets up to mischief. He wouldn't know what's right or wrong, would he, if I didn't?'

'No, Tracy,' agreed Clare. 'I dare say he wouldn't.'

'I try saying 'no', miss, but it don't work. Not with a tiny kid like that. No's only a word, isn't it? Words don't mean much really, do they? But a slap, that's different.'

'You don't live at home with your parents, do you, Tracy?' Clare asked, reading through the notes in her file.

'No, miss.' The answer came out in almost a whisper.

'Why not? Won't they have you? Is it because of the baby?'

Tracy shook her head. 'I wouldn't stay, miss. Not with me dad around.'

'Why not, Tracy?'

'Because he's a brute, miss.'

'Did he ever hit you?' The question was gentle.

'Hit us? He never stopped. Tony, Jacky, me . . . and our mum. When he's had a few, that is.'

'Your father drinks? Is he an alcoholic?'

Tracy looked at her in surprise as if she couldn't believe such an obvious question. ''Course he drinks, miss. Spends all his time in the boozer, 'cept when he's down the betting-shop.'

Clare sighed. It was quite a common fact that battered children often became, in the future, parents who battered their own children. So what hope did Tracy have? It was the pattern of her life.

'Where do you live now, Tracy?'

'Me and Dave's got a room in Trarrant Street.'

Clare knew the street well. A row of dilapidated Victorian terraces in a bad state of repair, bought up by a property dealer and let out at ridiculous rents to any desperate and homeless soul who was in no position to complain.

They should have been pulled down years ago, but while the town had a housing problem, it was unlikely that anything would be done. At least it kept people from sleeping under bridges.

'Is Dave Jamie's father, Tracy?'

The girl looked at her and smiled for the first time.

''Course not, miss. My Jamie's white as you are.'

'And Dave isn't?'

Tracy shook her head. 'He's a great guy though, for all he's not Jamie's real dad.'

'Is Dave working? Does he keep you and Jamie?'

Tracy's eyes were downcast again, her shoulders tight and hunched.

'Sort of.'

'Has he got a record? Has he ever been in prison, Tracy?'

She nodded without looking up, her thin body tensing.

'What did he go to prison for?'

A horrible feeling was beginning to creep into Clare now.

Tracy didn't answer, her fingers twisting a scrap of tissue round and round until it disintegrated and fell into a scatter of tiny pieces on the floor.

'Is Dave the one who hits Jamie?' she

questioned gently.

'No, miss!' The words burst out in a wild protest as Tracy jumped to her feet and made for the door, struggling with the handle. When she'd opened it, she turned, her small face defiant.

'He wouldn't do that, miss. Not Dave.'

'Tell me his surname, Tracy. I'll have to make a check on him.'

'You won't get him into no trouble, will you, miss? Dave's been good to me. Please, miss . . . I don't want to lose him.' The tears were back again, trickling down her face in thin rivers.

'His name, Tracy.'

'Watts, miss. Dave Watts. But he wouldn't do no harm, miss. Not to my Jamie. He wouldn't do that.'

Going back to her desk after Tracy had gone, Clare felt drained. It wouldn't be the first time. Live-in boyfriend, jealous of the attention the child was getting. A lively child, too. All sleeping in one room.

No, thought Clare sadly, it wasn't an

unusual reason for a child to be battered.

★　★　★

Geoffrey's mouth closed over hers as he pulled the car into the shadows of the trees, his hands sliding down over her shoulders.

'Oh, Clare, I don't know how I've managed to keep away from you all day, darling.'

'I thought we were going for a meal, Geoffrey.'

'Who needs a meal when I've got you all to myself like this?'

She caught his questing hands and pushed them away, aware of the annoyed expression in his eyes as she did so.

'Come on, Clare. You're getting to be as bad as Eileen. That's the kind of thing she does. What's the matter with you?'

'Nothing,' Clare replied, 'but it's been a busy day. If we're not going to eat, then I'd like to go home if you don't mind.'

'I do mind,' he said, shaking off her restricting fingers. 'You know why I brought you here. Can't you at least pretend to enjoy it?'

'Well, I'm not,' Clare retorted angrily. 'I'm fed up with this hole-in-corner affair. A year ago you told me you were leaving your wife. You no longer loved each other, you said. You led completely separate lives. She understood, you said, so there'd be no difficulty in getting a divorce. I'd never have gone out with you in the first place if I hadn't believed that, but it was all a lie, wasn't it?'

'How else does one get a girl like you? And, anyway, don't tell me you weren't intelligent enough to read between the lines.'

There was a sneer in his voice that stung her.

'What would you do if I said I was leaving the firm?'

'You have a contract of employment, Clare. It binds you for six months.'

'And if I broke that contract?'

'I'd make damn sure you never got another job in the legal profession.'

Leaning back, Clare breathed deeply, wondering, not for the first time, why she'd let herself get so involved.

'Look, Clare.' Geoffrey reached out and touched her hair lightly. 'Stop being silly. You're tired, I know that, and I do appreciate your workload is getting a bit too much for you, but darling, we'll soon be together in that little hotel. You'll be more relaxed then — right away from everything. Things will be quite different in Suffolk.'

So very different, thought Clare, remembering the peace and tranquillity of the little town there, the softness of the air, the smell of the sea, the breeze lifting her hair — and the aura of love that surrounded her wherever she went.

★　★　★

On her return home, she climbed the stairs wearily, throwing her jacket onto

113

the sofa as she passed, and paused, looking down at the telephone on the low polished table, wanting desperately to hear Neal's voice again.

It was late. He would be eating, or maybe walking along the shore in the evening sunset. He wouldn't be there.

Her hand reached out — and then she remembered she didn't even know his number.

After a pause, she dialled.

'Uncle Bill? It's Clare.'

'You'll want your Aunt Margaret then,' came the quiet voice and she could imagine her uncle placing his pipe carefully down in the ashtray beside the telephone and turning to go into the kitchen.

'No, Uncle Bill. I want to speak to you.'

'Me?' Surprise echoed in her ear.

'You remember John's best man at the wedding? Neal. Do you have his phone number? I . . . ' She hesitated, trying to think up an excuse. 'I need to consult him on a legal matter.'

Uncle Bill gave a chuckle. 'Legal matter, is it? Oh, I dare say I can find his number for you if it's a *legal* matter, Clare. Wait a bit. Yes, here we are — 65452. That's his home number though. Did you want his office?'

'No, that'll do fine,' Clare replied, quickly writing it down.

'Are you keeping well?'

'I'm fine,' she replied.

'Well, goodbye then, my dear.'

'Goodbye, Uncle Bill. And thanks.'

★   ★   ★

Her fingers trembled and she misdialled once before the ringing-tone murmured in her ears. He wouldn't be there, she knew.

'65452.'

She breathed slowly, trying to keep her voice steady.

'Neal?'

'Hullo, Clare.' He sounded surprised.

There was a pause. What did she say now?

'Are you still there?'

'Yes, Neal.'

All she wanted was to listen to him, feel the calmness that he seemed to evoke, even so far away.

'Is something the matter?'

'No.' Her brain was racing now. 'Well, yes. I want to ask your advice,' she said breathlessly.

'My advice? Well, well. I am honoured.'

He was mocking her again.

'Okay then. Ask away.'

'It's just that . . . I need someone to discuss a case with independently. Someone with an unbiased opinion. What I mean is . . . '

She stopped. What did she mean?

'What you mean is you want to air your views and see if I agree with them? Is that it?'

'More or less.'

'Right. I'll just sir here quietly and listen.'

'I'm dealing with a rather difficult case . . . ' Clare began, and told him about Tracy and Jamie.

'You see,' she concluded, 'I don't think Tracy does hit the child. It could be the boyfriend though, but how do I get her to admit it? She's desperate not to lose Jamie. It would crucify her if she did. He's the one thing she has that really belongs to her. The one thing in her pathetic life she can be sure of.'

'Have you got any details about the boyfriend?' Neal asked.

'Yes, but they're not good, I'm afraid. Grievous bodily harm. Assault. Robbery with violence.'

'Have you met him?'

'No. Do you think I should? I must admit I hadn't considered that. Would it help?'

'Well, you'd see first-hand how he reacts when you broach the subject with him, and also what he's like with this girl Tracy. I always find you can judge a person far better by meeting and talking to them. Police records often look pretty grim in black and white, but once you actually get to know the person concerned, sometimes there's a very good reason.'

There was a silence as if he was considering, then his voice continued: 'Can you have a word with him and the girl together? How about popping round to their home. I know it's not exactly going by the book, but if you can see what conditions they live under, maybe it would give you a better insight into their way of life.'

'Thanks, Neal. You've been a great help. I hope you didn't mind me phoning?'

'Any time.'

She could imagine that mocking smile playing round his lips.

'I'm always prepared to help a damsel in distress — and you certainly sound rather distressed, Clare. Is this case getting to you?'

'Of course not,' she replied brusquely. 'It's just as I said, I needed an unbiased opinion.'

She thought she heard him laugh softly, guessing he'd read her mind only too clearly yet again.

'It's a beautiful night here, Clare. I can see the moon like a huge glowing bowl over the sea, making a path of silver right back to the shore.'

His voice was low. 'Don't you wish you were here so that we could walk out along it and vanish into the unknown together?'

'It sounds as if we'd get very wet — once again.'

'Sorry, I keep forgetting you're not a romantic.'

'And never likely to be,' Clare informed him swiftly. 'Anyway, thanks for your advice. 'Bye.'

Not a romantic, he'd said.

So why were her dreams that night filled with visions of a tall, dark, handsome man on a beach bathed in moonlight, the air adrift with floating thistledown? And why did she feel his mouth warm on hers, his arms holding her close, his eyes no longer teasing as they gazed deep into her own?

6

'Where are you going?' Geoffrey asked her when he came into the office the next afternoon and found her putting on her jacket.

'I'm going round to see Tracy Francis.'

'What on earth for? You've read the reports, haven't you? Either she or that boyfriend of hers battered the child. The case is quite clear-cut. There's nothing more for you to bother about. The child's been removed. What more do you want?'

'But supposing they didn't do it? What then? Tracy worships that little boy and he quite genuinely adores her too. Would that happen if she'd beaten him? He's a lively child, Geoffrey. These things happen. Think about Jonathan. How did he fracture his arm?'

'That's quite different, Clare. Jonathan fell off his bike.'

'Has he ever broken any bones before?'

'There was his wrist. He was only a baby then and tumbled out of his high-chair. And once he suffered slight concussion when his pram tipped.'

'See what I mean,' Clare cried triumphantly.

'Maybe if he'd been from a one-parent family, living in a squalid little room, instead of the son of a wealthy solicitor in a six-bedroomed mansion, someone at the hospital might have started asking questions.'

Geoffrey's face changed slightly and he gave her a penetrating look, then said abruptly, 'I'll come with you.'

That wasn't exactly what Clare had in mind. She didn't fancy Geoffrey breathing down her neck while she was interviewing such a nervous person as Tracy, but with him being her superior, she didn't have a great deal of choice.

The house was one of a long terrace, paint peeling from the window-sills, grass waist-high in the garden, a couple of old cars lying in rusty pieces half-buried amongst what had once been a lawn. The narrow road outside was filled with a horde of children on skateboards and bikes.

A stale smell of cats, cabbage and curry met them as they opened the front door and began to climb the dirty carpetless stairs. Music echoed round them mingled with the sound of raised voices and wailing babies.

What chance do people have in conditions like this? Clare thought, stepping over piles of beer cans and rubbish strewn along the bare boards of the wooden landing. The open door of a toilet yawned, revealing the filthy condition of the small room, its wash-basin cracked, taps dripping.

Geoffrey's nose wrinkled in disgust and he banged hard on one of the doors.

A stubble-shaded dark-skinned face peered cautiously round the edge as it opened.

'Is Tracy there, Dave?' Clare asked, pushing forward before the door could close again. 'It's me, Tracy. Clare Darley. I want to talk to you about Jamie.'

The door was instantly jerked wide and Tracy's thin little face stared back at them, her eyes searching the landing outside.

'Where is he? Have you got him?'

'Can we come in, Tracy?'

The small face crumpled with disappointment as they went into the shabby room. In one corner was a bed, neatly made, its covers clean, although old and faded. A scratched but polished table and four leather-seated chairs, carefully mended with tape, were in the other corner, with a squashed-looking sofa against one wall. Nothing more.

At least she tries to keep it clean, thought Clare, sitting down on one of the chairs.

'When's my Jamie coming home, miss?'

'I don't know yet, Tracy, but that's what Mr Williams and I want to talk to you and Dave about, to see if we can try to sort things out properly, then we can decide what's going to happen.'

'Right then, Dave,' Geoffrey began, leaning over him. 'I gather you have a prison record. Some form of violence, isn't it?'

The young man drew back, his face tightening.

'Look, Dave,' said Clare quickly, 'I know Jamie's a bit of a handful, but it must be difficult, living in such a confined space. How did you get on with him?'

'We got on fine. He's a bright little kid.'

'Dave used to take Jamie out to the park — there's swings and slides and everything there — isn't there, Dave?' piped Tracy, her voice rising into a high note of panic.

The lad nodded, his arm moving to

rest gently round the girl's fragile shoulders.

Clare studied them closely, noticing the way his fingers were making a soothing movement along her reed-like neck, trying to calm her.

'It's all right, Trace. Don't get all upset. We'll get him back.' The dark eyes turned to Clare. 'We will get him back, won't we?'

'I hope so, Dave.'

'You were the one who beat the boy, weren't you? You might as well confess.' Geoffrey's voice was full of purpose. 'It's quite obvious. A man with a record like you've got. The best thing would be for you to collect your things and move out of here right this minute. In that way we might stand a chance of getting the child back to his mother.'

Tracy's fingers gripped at Dave's white tee-shirt, her eyes filling with more tears.

'No!' she sobbed. 'Dave never touched him, mister. He never did. Nor did I.

Not to hurt him bad like they said.'

'So you admit you did hit him,' said Geoffrey triumphantly.

'Did Jamie ever fall, Dave?' Clare put in, frowning a swift warning, trying to ease a situation that was rapidly growing out of hand. 'When you were in the playground perhaps?'

She remembered the way the little boy had behaved in her office, racing round, climbing up the filing-cabinet, delving into everything, filled with curiosity.

''Course he did. Always tripping over his own feet he was. A bit pigeon-toed if you ask me. Little kids like that often are.'

Geoffrey opened his mouth to speak and Clare stepped hard on his foot, seeing him flinch with pain, but for once he took her hint and was silent.

'Tracy, if you had to go into court and swear on the Bible that neither you nor Dave had beaten Jamie, could you do that? It would mean you had to be telling the honest truth?'

'Like crossing me heart, wish to die?' she questioned, her face anxious and pinched with fear.

'Just like that,' replied Clare.

'Yes,' Tracy answered firmly.

'And that Dave didn't hurt him either?'

There was no hesitation. 'He didn't, miss. Honest and true, he didn't.'

★ ★ ★

'Well, what did you make out of all that?' Geoffrey asked, as they picked their way back down the dirt-strewn stairs.

'I think she was telling the truth.'

'Well, I still think that young ruffian did it. He's got a record, Clare.'

'Not for hitting young children. And besides, the last time he was inside was over eighteen months ago. He's been with Tracy ever since then. I think he's trying to go straight and he seems to be succeeding. All that happened when he was in his teens, Geoffrey. He was in

127

with a bad crowd then. There were gangs of hooligans roaming round where he lived, just looking for trouble, and if they couldn't find anything, they started a rumpus themselves. It was a case of joining in, or be beaten up instead.'

'So why this sympathy for Dave when Ed Booker is no different?'

'Ed Booker is rotten through and through. He's thoroughly evil. He'll never change. One day he'll commit murder, just you wait and see.'

She climbed into the Rover, pulling on the seatbelt, and waited until Geoffrey had eased the car away from the kerb, avoiding a group of boys aiming stones at an empty can in the middle of the road.

'I really think Dave's over the worst,' she continued. 'Tracy's a dear little thing and she needs someone to look after her. She's another one who's never had a chance but who's trying to break away from her old life.'

'My, my, Clare. You're quite a

crusader, aren't you?' Geoffrey's voice was tinged with sarcasm.

'Am I? Well, I do feel very strongly about this sort of thing. There are some who really need all the help they can get. It's so easy for them to fall backwards again. What chance do they have? Look at that place where Dave and Tracy live. Compare your children's life with that of young Jamie.'

'Once a criminal, always a criminal, Clare. You're just wasting your time bothering with people like that. It's far better the child is brought up by foster-parents or in a children's home. He'll live a much happier — and probably far safer — life.'

'How can you say that? What about his mother? She loves him. He loves her too. How can you separate them? It isn't right.'

'And neither is it right that the child should be sent back to be beaten again, Clare. Obviously this case is getting to you. You're becoming too emotionally involved and it's clouding your judgment. From now on, I'm taking it over.'

'No, Geoffrey!' she protested.

'Yes, Clare,' he said firmly.

★   ★   ★

The hotel was, as Geoffrey had told her, a secluded one, set in a little village down by the edge of the estuary. Looking across in the bright afternoon sunshine, she could see the town where her aunt and uncle lived quite clearly, its church spire rising over the dark roofs of the houses, and felt very guilty. They'd be terribly disappointed if they knew she was so close, yet hadn't come to stay with them.

Geoffrey was arriving later that evening. He'd left the office earlier in the day, saying he'd meet her there.

'It's better we shouldn't be seen driving off together, darling. People do talk so,' he explained.

Clare really couldn't see why it should matter. They were going to the same conference. Surely it was more convenient, and also cheaper for the firm, if they travelled in the same car? But in the end she agreed. Geoffrey always seemed worried that Eileen was going to discover their relationship. Why, Clare couldn't see. Nothing had happened between them — yet.

She wasn't even sure it would.

Gazing out over the estuary, she wondered whether she should phone Neal. Since that call a couple of weeks before, she'd heard nothing from him. But then, why should she? She'd refused his proposal of marriage and no man, especially one like Neal, would welcome that.

But, somehow, she wished he had been more persistent. It rather surprised her that he hadn't.

She was forgetting though — he'd been married before — and it had ended. Perhaps his wife wasn't able to live with such a single-minded man. Clare wondered which of them had left the other.

And perhaps, now, he couldn't take rejection.

And yet there was a kindness and gentleness about him that seemed to belie such an overbearing nature.

Or maybe Nicola's wedding had had a mellowing effect on him too that weekend and she'd seen him in a rare light.

Anyway, she thought, as she hung a couple of light dresses in the old-fashioned wardrobe standing in one corner of the room, I'm here with Geoffrey and the next few days are going to decide my future one way or another.

Yet she could feel no enthusiasm or excitement at the idea.

When the telephone rang in her room a few minutes later, her heart missed a beat. Could it be?

'Clare. You're never going to forgive me, darling.'

Geoffrey's silky tones quivered down the line.

'Where are you? Are you held up

somewhere?' Clare asked.

'It's one of the boys, darling. He's gone down with mumps. There's no way Eileen can cope on her own. The other one's sure to catch it too.'

'What are you trying to tell me, Geoffrey?'

'There's no way I can come up to Suffolk, darling. You'll just have to attend the conference on your own. Make plenty of notes, won't you and we'll go over them when you get back.'

'Did you know about the mumps when you went home suddenly?' Clare questioned.

'Of course not, darling. Why should I?'

A good solicitor must always be able to lie convincingly, Clare remembered him saying to her.

'Then why did you leave early?'

'I had to pack, darling.' There was a slight bluster in his voice.

'But you already had your case with you. Don't you remember? You gave me some files you'd been working on from it when you arrived this morning.'

'Ah, yes . . . But I'd forgotten one of my suits. You know, the grey lightweight one. The weather could turn much warmer.'

'Are you quite sure it isn't because Eileen objected? When she discovered you were going with me, she made a fuss? Despite appearing so passive and wishy-washy, Eileen rules you completely, doesn't she, Geoffrey? You're totally under her thumb. There's no way you'll ever leave her, is there?'

Clare felt a wave of fury roar over her.

'Why do you carry on all this pretence? That 'my wife doesn't understand me' routine is so outdated. Why not be honest? Why not admit you like a little fling with the latest female in the office; that you enjoy the challenge, the feeling of power?'

'Clare! Darling!'

She slammed down the receiver and hoped it deafened him.

How could she have been so stupid? All these months. She knew what the girls in the office said about him. She'd heard it all and chosen to ignore it. What was the matter with her?

Why had she let herself be taken in?

A handsome, wealthy, mature man. A man like the father she'd once adored. The same smoothness, the same flattering charm. The way he, too, could win over any woman — even her. As a child she had worshipped her father, despising her mother for the angry taunts she threw at him. How could anyone be so cruel to such an adorable man, she had wondered.

And then, as she grew older, she began to understand. Realising just how much her mother must have suffered over the years, knowing his infidelities, the endless string of other women, growing younger all the time as he himself grew older.

She remembered the trauma when he finally went away, seeing her mother's tears, but even then she still loved him, wanting to go with him, feeling his rejection cut into her like a knife.

In a way she loved him still. He was her father.

Did that mean she'd merely transferred that love to someone like Geoffrey, in the hope of gaining what she'd lost all those years ago — the love of a father?

But it only proved even more strongly to her that marriage was a travesty. A mockery of the word love.

She wondered again what sort of marriage Neal had once — and why it ended.

She was glad he was in London. Glad there wasn't the chance of accidentally meeting him. She wasn't sure what would happen if she saw those caring eyes again, heard that calm voice, felt the soothing touch of his hands. She was glad he was in London.

So why was she crying?

★   ★   ★

The conference was an intensive one. Lectures and seminars all day, every

136

day. Clare took endless notes. Conveyancing was a complex subject. She hadn't realised that the buying and selling of a house could have so many pitfalls.

On one afternoon there was an outing. To Minsmere.

What was the point of going, Clare thought. She'd been there before. Lakes. Wildfowl. They wouldn't change.

In the sunshine everything was different. The reeds were a deeper green. Colours she never imagined could exist were revealed in the plumage of the birds. Black wasn't just black but a combination of iridescent green and blue. Feathers that looked a drab brown revealed cinnamon and gold flecks. Gossamer-winged dragon-flies swooped low over the unruffled surface of the water in a rainbow shimmer of colour. Even the muddy water of the lakes glinted and sparkled as the sun caught it.

But without Neal there beside her, explaining things, pointing out details she would never have noticed, there wasn't the same enjoyment.

She was sitting silently in one of the hides, hearing the waves pound against the pebbles of the beach, seeing puffball clouds drift lazily across the clear blue sky, when she sensed rather than saw him.

The wooden door creaked open behind her, letting in a shaft of brightness, a breath of salt-laden air. Dusty boards echoed with footsteps.

Someone was bending to sit beside her.

She breathed once more the faint smell of that elusive aftershave; the tweed of his jacket.

It couldn't be . . .

Clare turned her head reluctantly and felt her heart lurch sideways when she saw him smile.

7

'I thought you were in London,' she said.

'The case was adjourned. The petitioner's solicitor was unable to attend. There was no need to go.'

He paused, looking down into her eyes as if he couldn't tear his own away from her.

'I tried to phone your flat. There was no reply.'

'I've been here since Tuesday,' she told him. 'I'm at a conference nearby. They organised an outing here today . . . I didn't want to come.'

His eyes still gazed into hers as though penetrating the very depths of her soul. 'Why? Did you hate it so much before? If so, I'm sorry.'

'Oh no,' she replied hastily. 'It wasn't that.'

Why couldn't she tell him that

without him, the place held no magic for her, that now he was there too, everything would be different . . .

'Will you have dinner with me, Clare?'

She hesitated. 'The others . . . I should get back . . . '

'Always an excuse,' he sighed. 'Why not be honest, Clare? You hate my guts, don't you?'

Hate him? How could she hate him?

'I'd love to have dinner with you, Neal.'

★   ★   ★

It was an old pub down near the sea, its view reaching far away to the horizon. Grey and yellow lichen was thick upon the slated roof, its diamond-paned windows hazed with salt. The heavy beams were cracked and low, the walls rough and unevenly plastered. Polished dark wooden tables part-filled the room, silver gleamed, scarlet napkins tucked into shining glasses. It had a restful intimate atmosphere. It was a place for lovers.

Neal handed her the menu.

'You choose,' she said.

'Me? Choose for you? What's the matter, Clare? Somehow this isn't like you — allowing a man to make a decision.'

Not again. Please, Clare thought desperately, not again. Don't let him spoil things by mocking me. Why, oh why did it always happen?

He leaned across the table, lifting her chin with gentle fingers, making her gaze meet his eyes.

'I'm sorry, Clare. I shouldn't tease you. I know how much you hate it.'

'Reading my thoughts again?' she challenged, and saw him smile. 'What was the word you used? Affinity?'

'Or maybe love,' he said quietly. 'But love isn't something you wish to know about, is it, Clare? Now, tell me about your conference. I'd heard there was one, but I didn't book as I thought I'd be in London then. Are you the only one representing your firm or are there others?'

'There should have been two of us. One of the partners and me. He couldn't come at the last minute. One of his sons has gone down with mumps, so he had to stay at home.'

'Why, is he in quarantine or something?'

Clare shook her head. 'I don't think so. Do people bother about quarantine any more?'

She looked directly at him as she continued: 'To be honest I think his wife objected to me being there too.'

There was a pause while the waitress brought their meal, carefully spooning green beans, cauliflower and roast potatoes onto their plates from a long silver dish, then tipping a stream of thick rich gravy over slices of rarely-cooked beef.

'It was to have been a testing time,' Clare said slowly.

Neal's dark eyes studied her closely. 'For you?'

'For both of us, I suppose. I think he got cold feet in the end.' Clare gave a brittle laugh. 'For him it was probably just an interlude, a slight variation on a theme.'

'But for you it was serious?'

Clare considered the question.

Serious? Had it ever been? Or was it merely because she was flattered at being singled out by someone so mature and sophisticated? A man who could influence the whole future of her job. She, of all people, who held such strong views too.

'No,' she replied at last. 'I don't think it would ever have been serious. Love's an emotion far too powerful to let myself succumb to.'

'But why? Surely everyone falls in love? It's a natural part of life.'

'Love is something too tenuous, too fragile, to risk. Hearts are too easily broken,' she said, looking at him, her green eyes half-hidden by thick lashes. 'If you don't fall in love, you can't be hurt, can you?'

'Why are you so frightened, Clare?'

She stared back at him in the flickering candlelight, studying the strong planes of his face, the slight cleft in a square chin that emphasised the curving width of his mouth and finally, reluctantly, met the caring depths of his eyes.

Frightened?

The word startled her.

Was she frightened? Frightened of being in love; of revealing the inner depths of her soul to another; of letting someone else be in control of her, of her life?

Was she frightened?

'You're beautiful, Clare.' Neal was leaning across the table towards her, his fingers touching hers. She dared not meet his eyes, terrified of what her own would reveal.

There was a strangeness about her, a light-headed feeling that had nothing to do with the wine, an uplifting of her spirit, almost as if she was floating . . . like thistledown.

A thistledown feeling. Was this what Nicky meant? Could it mean that she, too, was falling in love?

Had fallen in love maybe?

The low arched door of the restaurant burst open and a noisy group of people came in, filling the bar. Clare saw to her dismay that they were all from the conference, already rather drunk — and amongst them was Geoffrey.

'Clare, darling,' he slurred, lurching across the room towards her. 'So this is what you get up to once my back is turned.'

His glance flickered over Neal, taking in their closeness.

'I thought . . . ' Clare began.

'You thought I was safely tied to Eileen's apron-strings, didn't you, darling? But I just couldn't keep away from you, could I?'

'What about Jonathan?'

'Jonathan? Don't talk to me about that wretched child. It wasn't mumps at all, darling. A septic tooth all the time.

145

Once gone, all better. Now, darling, what are you drinking?'

'I'm fine, thank you, Geoffrey.'

She drew back from the fumes on his breath.

'Nonsense. Another bottle of whatever that stuff is, waitress. Don't mind if I join you, do you, old chap?'

Without waiting for an answer, Geoffrey dragged across a chair and placed it next to Clare, his arm sliding round her shoulders, caressing the slender column of her neck, his fingers tightening as she tried to move away, her face beginning to burn.

She was aware of the hostility in Neal's eyes as he watched them, a twitching nerve in his cheek revealing his anger.

'Drink up, darling. I want you warm and mellow for tonight.'

Geoffrey's bleary gaze turned to Neal. 'Sorry, but I've got first priority, old chap. Been waiting for this for months now. Don't want to miss out.'

'I think we'd better leave, Neal.'

Clare rose to her feet, picking up her bag.

'Are you quite sure?'

There was no mistaking the irony in his voice as he looked at her.

'Quite sure,' she replied firmly.

'But darling, what about us? You're not going to desert me so soon?'

Geoffrey's hands clutched at her dress, then his slack mouth opened in a leer.

'Ah, impatient to get back to the hotel, is that it, darling? I won't keep you waiting long.'

Stiffening her back, Clare pushed past his outstretched legs and hurried to the door, conscious of a sudden silence and every eye in the room turned upon her.

'I'm sorry, Neal,' she apologised once they were outside in the cool night air of the shadowy car-park.

'I presume you know him,' Neal remarked.

'Geoffrey's a partner in the firm. I work for him.'

'So he's the one you were coming here with. I'm sorry if I spoilt things.' His tone was cold. 'Maybe I was wrong about you after all. Maybe you're not the ice-maiden you appear to be, but made of fire after all. Geoffrey would already know that, I imagine.'

Clare caught at his sleeve, hating to see the look in his dark eyes.

'Nothing has ever happened between us, Neal.'

'Yet.' The single word sounded like the ricochet of a bullet.

'It won't happen either, Neal.'

'No wonder you're always so distant.' Neal slammed the car door and wrenched the engine into life. 'I should've realised there was someone else. A beautiful and intelligent girl like you must have a trail of admirers. Nicky said as much when she spoke about you before the wedding. It used to make her jealous, she said.'

'Now you are being stupid.' Clare's green eyes sparked with anger, her red hair flaring backwards in the rush of air

148

as the open car tore down the winding lanes, tyres screeching round each bend when Neal savagely swung the steering-wheel.

Outside the conference centre, he held open the door and waited until she swung her slender legs over the side.

'Goodnight, Clare. Don't keep your lover waiting.'

'Will I see you again?'

Her voice was pleading.

'I doubt it. There won't be any need to do so, will there?'

With a grinding crunch of the gears, the car spun round sending up a spray of gravel, before tearing off down the drive.

Clare stood watching, waiting, but Neal's head didn't turn.

* * *

When the lock clicked and the handle of her bedroom door rattled later that night, Clare stirred slightly in her sleep.

When it creaked open she woke and

sat up, suddenly alarmed.

Geoffrey stood there, swaying, silhouetted in the moonlight that streamed in through her window.

'What do you want?'

He gave a long low laugh.

'What a stupid question, Clare.'

His voice was thick and slow, and the smell of whisky on his breath filled the room.

'Please leave.'

With stumbling footsteps, he lurched across the carpet and fell heavily onto the bed, his hands dragging away the covers.

'I said, will you leave my room.' Clare tried to sound calm.

'Your room. My room. Our room. What does it matter. I've been waiting months for this moment. Surely you're not going to play hard to get now, Clare?'

His fingers were gripping her shoulders, tearing at the flimsy material of her nightdress.

She tried to scream but no sound

came from her tense arched throat.

One of his hands slid over her bare breast and she heard the intake of his breath, then his mouth closed over hers, wet and foul-tasting.

With a rush of anger that gave her courage, she pounded her fists hard against his chest, trying to push him away, but his strength was too much for her and she could feel the softness of the pillow as he forced her backwards.

In fury her teeth clamped down onto his thrusting tongue, biting hard into it, and she felt his head jerk away as he cried out in pain and frustration.

'You little vixen!' he grunted, wiping his lips with the back of his hand to brush away the blood.

Freed of the weight of his body, Clare moved sideways in the bed and reached for the phone, picking up the receiver with shaking fingers.

'Either you leave my room now or I call the manager to remove you.'

Geoffrey laughed mockingly at her.

'And what would you tell him? Rape?

Indecent assault? Do you honestly think he'd believe you? Really, Clare. I thought you'd dealt with enough cases to realise the difficulty of making an accusation like that stick.'

He lunged towards her again breathing heavily.

Clare began to dial.

'All right. All right. I'll go, but there's no way I'm every going to forget this. No way at all.'

'And neither will I,' Clare retorted.

Feeling her legs begin to crumple under her, she sank onto a chair when the door slammed shut behind him, and burst into unaccustomed tears.

How could she ever face him again?

She couldn't continue to work with him after this. Geoffrey didn't appear at breakfast on that final day, whether from embarrassment or a hangover, she didn't know, but it was a great relief.

When she did meet him again, she could only be amazed at his outstanding bluff — or was it total amnesia? Had he been so drunk, he honestly didn't remember a thing that had happened? It hardly seemed possible.

'Sleep well, Clare?' he enquired, greeting her in the lecture-room for the first session. 'No disturbed dreams, I hope?'

'How can you ask that,' she burst out, 'after your behaviour last night?'

'My behaviour?'

A look of genuine puzzlement filled his expression.

'Coming into my room like you did.'

Surely he wasn't going to pretend it had never happened?

'You imbibed too much wine, my dear,' he laughed, patting her arm. 'Who was that handsome young fellow you were dining with, by the way?'

'He's a solicitor. He lives here in Suffolk. I met him at my cousin's wedding.'

Why am I telling him all this, she thought, appalled.

'I expect an apology, Geoffrey.'

'An apology, my dear! But for what?'

His jowled cheeks almost quivered

153

with bewildered indignation.

'For trying to rape me, Geoffrey.'

'Really, my dear. Such wishful thinking.'

His heavy shoulders shook with laughter and he turned to the man about to sit down beside him.

'Young women nowadays are so amazing, aren't they, Charles? You wouldn't think in this day and age they'd accuse a man of rape when they do all the running, would you?'

He turned back to Clare again.

'You must remember I'm a happily married man with a delightful wife and family, my dear.'

She felt her cheeks burn at his bantering tone and the skilful way he was turning the tables on her. He certainly had perfected that ability to lie.

He took a leather case from his pocket and slipped on a pair of thick-rimmed spectacles, then consulted his programme.

'There's been a change of speaker, I

gather. Old Haslett's got a touch of gout, poor chap. Some young local has stepped in at the last minute to take his place.'

Chairs scraped and papers rustled as the lecturer took the platform. Clare glanced up, startled to meet Neal's stony glare, seeing his eyes turn to Geoffrey sitting close beside her.

Then he began to speak.

Clare was impressed. She couldn't fail to be. Neal knew his subject inside out, conveying information with practised ease and dealing with the numerous and complicated questions that came at the end of his lecture without any hesitation.

When the gong sounded for lunch she waited, hoping he would come and speak to her, but he turned away without even a glance in her direction.

Throughout lunch she sat, hardly touching her food, her eyes following his every movement on the other side of the room. Some she knew so well now: the inclination of his dark head as he made a point; the slight raising of his eyebrows as he listened intently; the quirk of his mouth when he laughed.

Everything was so familiar it made her ache, wanting to be near to him, to touch those gesturing hands, to see the smile in his eyes when he looked at her.

But he totally ignored her, not even glancing across, although he must have been perfectly aware of her sitting there.

She was conscious, too, of Geoffrey watching her and the slight ironic twist of his thick lips at seeing her unhappiness.

When the conference ended that afternoon, he insisted she travelled back with him, despite her protests. She sat in the smoothly moving Rover, stiff and silent beside him, hating every minute of the journey.

It was quite obvious that he had chosen to ignore the previous night's episode, if he remembered it at all, and she decided maybe that was the best way to view the whole thing. After all, nothing *had* happened.

'We really must consider your work-load when we get back, Clare. Have you sorted out Miss Milsom's will yet? It was extremely urgent.'

'It's a cruel will,' Clare declared angrily. 'She's worth half a million and yet she's leaving it all to some wretched cats' home, while her poor sister Katherine, who's devoted the last ten years to coping with her, will only get a couple of thousand. The wretched woman's even instructed the house is to be sold so Katherine won't even have a home of her own. How can anyone be so vindictive?'

'Everyone is entitled to bequeath their assets as they wish, Clare,' Geoffrey replied, skilfully guiding the car round a broken-down lorry that was blocking the road.

'But what about little Miss Katherine? She inherited nothing when their parents died, everything going to the eldest daughter, and for years now she's waited on that dreadful sister hand and foot.'

'Miss Milsom is in poor health, Clare. She suffers from high blood-pressure.'

'Poor health! No wonder! She's immensely fat and lazy, that's all. Quite content to let her sister clean and polish and keep that great house running single-handed while she sits around all day.'

'Well that's not our concern, Clare. What is important is whether Miss Milsom has signed the will yet. Has she?'

Clare nodded. 'I took it round there one day last week and witnessed it myself with one of her neighbours. Being a beneficiary, of course Miss Katherine couldn't do so, although whether the poor woman realises just what a pittance she'll receive, I dread to think.'

Geoffrey smiled. 'There'll be a nice fat percentage when we eventually do the probate. How much did you say the old lady is worth?'

'With the value of the house and

contents included, nearly half a million, I should imagine.'

'Then I shall be able to consider a new car any day now,' Geoffrey said enthusiastically.

'Miss Milsom isn't dead yet,' Clare pointed out drily.

'Almost, my dear. When I came away yesterday afternoon, she'd just had a severe stroke. I think you can quite safely start preparing to do the probate.'

Miss Milsom died at five-thirty the following morning, making sure even with her death that she created as much inconvenience as possible for her sister Katherine.

However, when Clare phoned with her condolences, Miss Katherine sounded quite cheerful. Perhaps the shock had not yet sunk in, Clare decided.

'About probate,' she said gently.

'Oh, I shall want you to continue dealing with everything as usual, my dear,' Miss Katherine hastened to assure her. 'It's what Margaret would have wanted, I'm quite certain.'

'Then would you let me have her will? Your sister decided it should remain in her own safe-keeping, if you remember, rather than leave it here in our deed-safe.'

'Ah, the will.'

There was a slight pause.

'It shouldn't be difficult to find. It was a large manilla envelope, Miss Katherine, with LAST WILL typed in capital on the outside,' Clare reminded her.

'Yes, my dear, I know exactly what you are talking about. But there is a problem. You see, my sister tore it up.'

'Tore it up!'

'Well, you must admit it wasn't a very pleasant will, was it, my dear? Everything to that cats' home,' Miss Katherine declared indignantly. 'So Margaret changed her mind, considering it would be most unfair if the house and contents — plus enough for its upkeep, of course — should not come to me. After all, it is my home as well. I've lived here all my life — over seventy-five years now, you know.'

'Did your sister write out a new will?' Clare asked. 'She didn't mention anything to me. Maybe she spoke to Mr Williams but, if so, he didn't tell me, I'm afraid.'

'Oh no, my dear. She simply destroyed that one — the one you had drawn up so nicely — saying . . . now what was it she said? Let me see.'

There was a silence as if Miss Katherine was making certain of her facts.

'Ah yes, I remember. She said that if she died intestate — that is, without making a will — her estate automatically would come to me as her only surviving next of kin.'

'That's quite correct, Miss Katherine, but when did she do all this?'

'Soon after you'd gone, my dear. About an hour or so,' came the prompt reply. 'I think Margaret had a slight tremor of conscience, you know. Not an asset that my sister revealed very frequently, I'm afraid.'

Clare felt an unwelcome twinge of doubt. Miss Milsom had been so adamant at the time she dictated her instructions. The house and contents to be sold and the proceeds, together with her entire estate, to go to a certain cats' home in the town, apart from two thousand pounds which was to be given to her sister.

Clare had pointed out in vain that she was not being at all considerate for the welfare of Miss Katherine, but Miss Milsom had merely snorted and said it would make her sister stand on her own two feet and about time too.

She'd looked maliciously pleased as she said it too, and Clare thought what a spiteful old woman she was. It seemed strange she'd had a change of heart so soon after signing the document.

But people did have second thoughts, so there was no reason to think that Miss Milsom hadn't done the same. Miss Katherine was such a quiet, mild-natured little soul, full of kindness and quite devoted to looking after her elder sister, so it wasn't really surprising.

'Miss Katherine.'

'Yes, my dear.'

'I'm afraid you'll have to testify to what happened and swear an affidavit to that effect.'

'No trouble at all, my dear. You draw one up and I'll be along to sign it whenever you say.'

'It will mean swearing on the Bible, Miss Katherine,' Clare said gently, knowing what a devout church-goer she was.

'That will be quite all right, my dear,' Miss Katherine replied somewhat breathlessly. 'The dear Lord has always looked after me and I'm sure He will contine to do so. By the way, I should mention that the cremation is tomorrow.'

'So soon?'

'Yes, my dear. My sister always hated being kept waiting for anything. She would complain most bitterly to me if things didn't happen at once. She was not a patient woman, I'm afraid.'

'What time, Miss Katherine?'

'Two o'clock, my dear. I hope you'll be able to attend.'

Clare put the phone down thoughtfully. She didn't like the ideas whirling round in her head. Miss Katherine was a sweet little old lady. No way would she destroy her sister's will.

Or would she?

After all there was a great difference between the two thousand pounds she was due to receive and the entire estate which could amount to around half a million.

Had she decided to rebel at last after all the years of being dominated? It wouldn't be so surprising. Seventy-five years under her sister's unrelenting authority and anything could snap.

Miss Milsom's stroke had been very sudden.

Clare pushed the unpleasant thoughts away, but they kept creeping unwillingly back again.

Suppose, after she'd left that day and the will was signed, there'd been an argument. A sudden furious row. Miss Katherine, maybe learning from her spiteful sister the cruel instructions she'd left to be carried out after her death, defiantly tearing up the will in her face.

The sudden surge of fury it would provoke, in a woman whose heart was already under permanent strain from age and being extremely overweight, could prove to be fatal . . .

8

At one forty-five the next afternoon Clare arrived at the crematorium, suitably dressed in black. The service was a simple one.

She and Miss Katherine were the only people there.

There were no flowers.

'Margaret always considered them to be an extravagance, so I didn't bother,' explained Miss Katherine. 'I always had to follow her wishes during her lifetime, so there's no need to stop just because she's dead.'

Even the vicar's sermon was brief. He had never met the deceased until that day and was not likely to meet her again.

After they had shaken his hand in goodbye, Miss Katherine turned to Clare.

'Are you ready for me to swear that affidavit yet, my dear?' she questioned.

'It is typed, but I doubt you want to bother with it today of all days.'

'Whyever not?' Miss Katherine sounded surprised. 'I'd like to get it out of the way and off my conscience.'

'Well, if that's what you really want, we can go back to my office now.'

Miss Katherine had a taxi waiting. Expense was no longer a worry to her.

*　*　*

'Please read it carefully, Miss Katherine, and make sure that's exactly what happened,' Clare told her.

The old lady slipped on a pair of gold-rimmed glasses and studied the paper intently, her lips moving slightly as she read the words.

'Excellent. My sister Margaret tore up the will and expressed the desire for me to inherit her entire estate. That's exactly what happened. Now where do I sign?'

'We shall need to go across the road to Wilmington & Foster's. You'll have to swear it before a solicitor not connected with our firm, I'm afraid. It's one of the rules.'

*   *   *

'You are Katherine Josephine Milsom?' Mr Wilmington asked, blinking up at her through thick lenses, after he had carefully perused the document.

'I am.'

'You have read the contents of this affidavit and confirm they are true?'

Miss Katherine nodded quickly.

'Then take the Bible in your right hand and repeat after me, I Katherine Josephine Milsom do swear that the contents of this my affidavit . . . '

Clare noticed Miss Katherine's black gloved hand quiver slightly as she repeated the words in a solemn voice.

*   *   *

'Thank goodness that's over. Now you will come back for a cup of tea with me, won't you, my dear?'

Clare hesitated.

'Please.'

The waiting taxi-driver helped them into his gleaming vehicle, closed the door and began to drive silently along the road.

Miss Katherine settled herself comfortably against the padded seat and, with a contented smile, turned to Clare.

'I plan to sell the house and move near the sea, my dear. It's become rather a mausoleum, you know. Absolutely filled with memories of my sister. The past ten years have not been my happiest, since poor dear Father died, I'm afraid. I was beginning to turn into a very embittered old woman, you know, living with my sister, so I fully intend to enjoy the time that's left to me. You don't think that's very wicked, do you?'

She looked anxiously into Clare's green eyes.

'Of course not, Miss Katherine,'

Clare assured her, patting the gloved little hand.

'I shall of course make a donation to that cats' home. After all, it was my sister's desire that it should benefit. Two thousand pounds I feel would be quite appropriate, don't you? And I want you to deal with the house sale for me.'

She looked at Clare with a twinkle in her blue eyes.

'I'm going down to Brighton on Saturday to stay in an hotel on the sea-front, near to the Palace Pier. The air's so good there, don't you think? And there I shall remain until I find a suitable property in the area. One of those nice retirement flats they seem to be building everywhere maybe. Or perhaps a pretty little bungalow. I shall not be returning here again.'

'I hope everything works out well for you then, Miss Katherine.'

Miss Katherine gave her a satisfied glance.

'Oh, I'm sure it will ... now, my dear.'

Clare still had uneasy doubts when she returned to the office, especially when she remembered how Miss Katherine had not removed her gloves when she took the Bible.

Maybe she felt that if her hand wasn't actually in contact with its surface . . .

★   ★   ★

She was glad to get away to Suffolk that weekend on her promised visit to Aunt Margaret and Uncle Bill.

As the train flew along, passing the tiny patches of London gardens bordering the track before reaching the open fields and countryside, her heart pulsed in time to the rhythm of the wheels. Would she see Neal?

Nicky was there to meet her at the station, her face wearing a glow of contentment as she hugged her cousin.

'Well, how's married life?' Clare asked, and wished she hadn't when she saw the wide smile that beamed forth.

'Bliss,' her cousin sighed ecstatically.

'Still full of thistledown?'

'Was that what I said?' Nicola asked, looking surprised. 'I'm amazed I was so descriptive. But how are you, Clare?' She turned her head to study her cousin critically. 'You don't look quite so awful as before but maybe I'm getting used to the change in you.'

'Nicky! How can you be so rude?'

'You haven't put on any weight yet, but I'm glad to see you're not wearing that dreary black.'

'If you must know, I went out specially in my lunch-hour to buy this outfit,' Clare said, but didn't add that it was also in case she saw Neal again.

'It suits you,' replied Nicola, nodding approvingly at the gently flowing lines of the silky dress in soft shades of green and turquoise that highlighted Clare's auburn hair perfectly. 'I like that jacket too. It's a gorgeous colour — and it looks horribly expensive.'

Clare glanced down at the deep jade that toned with the dress, pleased with the comment. It *was* expensive. Even she had been taken aback when she learned the price.

And yet Nicola, she felt, in her faded lavender-blue tee-shirt and worn jeans, still looked even better.

'How's John?'

'Perfect.'

'No doubts any more?'

Nicola looked straight into her eyes and shook her head. 'No doubts at all. Married life couldn't be more wonderful. You really should try it. I'm sure Neal would be only too happy to oblige. He's always asking about you.'

'Is he?' Clare felt a bubble of delight rise up within her.

'He's quite obsessed with you, you know. I've never seen him like this before.'

'About his marriage ... ' Clare began, but Nicola was already swinging the car up to the little green outside her parents' house.

The front door opened instantly and

Clare knew that as usual they'd been watching for their arrival as they came swiftly down the path to meet her.

'Still missing Nicky?' Clare asked her aunt when they climbed the stairs to the pretty little room where she'd always slept since she was a little girl.

'Missing her? She's never out of the house!' laughed Aunt Margaret. 'We see more of her and John now than we did when they were off courting all the time. Always popping in and out they are. John's redecorating their cottage and so he's usually after some advice from Bill, and of course Nicky's never far behind.'

Clare remembered her last visit when they'd all sat down to tea, and hoped Neal would put in an appearance as well, but much to her disappointment he didn't and although she desperately wanted to, she couldn't bring herself to ask after him.

It was quite late when the newly-weds left, making her promise she'd be round at their new home early next morning to see what improvements they'd made.

She went out into the moonlit garden, feeling the dew-wet grass soft beneath her feet, savouring the night scents of stocks and roses. Uncle Bill loved his garden and it was always filled with colour and fragrance whatever time of year.

A light burned in the small shed he'd built at the end of the lawn, a haven of peace, she decided, to which he retired when Aunt Margaret's chatter became too much for him.

She remembered when she was a child finding him there, working away planing a piece of wood, or painting something, all on his own, hearing the tuneless whistle that came from his lips as he concentrated.

He was so different from her own father, so very different. She'd realised that even when she was quite young. Uncle Bill could never be called handsome with his rather angular and bony face from which the hair had

175

receded rapidly many years before, leaving a sparse ring of speckled grey above his ears.

His face had always been lined, but they were lines of kindness not discontent. Clare remembered how his eyes seemed to disappear when he smiled and his mouth always had a slight upward tilt, even when he was being serious. He was such a placid man, gentle, comforting.

She would sit on an upturned box, watching his deft fingers turning wood on a lathe, making salad and fruit bowls for a local craft-shop in the town, seeing the warm glow of the wood as he polished it. He rarely spoke, but just to be there in his company was entirely different from the effusive overwhelming personality of her own father.

Even then, all those years ago, she'd felt soothed just by being with him.

He looked up now as she knocked on the door of the shed, smiling at her in the glow of the light-bulb above his bench.

'Hullo, Clare.'

His roughened hands were polishing the base of a lampstand, the depth of shine almost burning in the sharpness of the light.

'Come for a chat, have you, my dear?'

She nodded.

'Tell me about Neal, Uncle Bill. Tell me about his marriage.'

The faded blue eyes looked up at her shrewdly. 'Missing him, are you?'

'Of course I'm not,' she replied sharply.

Then seeing the slight twitch to her uncle's lips, she said, 'Well, I did wonder if he'd be here too. He seemed almost a part of the family when I was here before.'

'He said he wouldn't come. You met him a while ago — at a conference, he said. I don't think he knows quite how to understand you, Clare.'

Her uncle's head was bent now, following the rhythmic movements of his hands on the wood.

'You can be a prickly little creature at

times, you know.'

'Did he say that?'

'He hinted as much,' smiled Uncle Bill. 'But I've known you a long time, Clare. You're become withdrawn over the past few years, you know, as if hiding from the world and your true feelings. Something's wrong, isn't it, my dear?'

'It's Neal I came to hear about,' she reminded him quickly.

Uncle Bill dipped his cloth into the beeswax he was using. 'Young Neal's marriage, is that what's worrying you?'

'All I know is that once he was married. What happened? Are they divorced?'

Uncle Bill shook his head.

'No. Anna died.'

'Died?'

'It was a tragic affair.'

'What happened?'

'He was devoted to that girl. Quite devoted, but sometimes I doubt she ever loved him at all.'

Clare waited for him to continue,

perching herself on the edge of his bench.

He gave a sigh. 'They were very young, both of them. Neal hadn't lived here long then. His father moved into the area when he bought the practice from Tom Winters when he retired. He hoped Neal would join him after he'd finished at university.'

'Was that where Neal met Anna?' Clare prompted.

'At university? Yes. Pretty little thing she was. Very slender. Blonde too. Full of vitality. Not the sort to be tied down to one man though. Neal brought her home a few times and then the next thing we all knew they were married.'

'Did they live here?'

'Oh no, Neal was still studying for his degree and Anna was taking art, I believe. She painted anyway. Often out on the marshes you'd see her, working away. Or swimming. She loved swimming. Like a mermaid she was. Swam like one too.'

He glanced up at Clare with a

twinkle in his eye. 'Quite naked.'

'I bet that shocked a few of the natives,' Clare commented, but felt a sudden pang of jealousy at the thought of anyone capturing Neal's attention in such a way.

'I somehow doubt she was faithful to Neal for more than a month or two after they were married though.'

He paused, smiling slightly as he remembered.

'She was like an elusive butterfly, flamboyant, delicate, never to be held. It wasn't long before she became the talk of the town, which wasn't fair to Neal who was away at law school by then.'

'So how did she die?'

'Drowned.'

'But you said she swam like a mermaid?'

'She did, but that was before she got involved with an arty group who came down that summer. They set up camp on the cliffs over near Dunwich. Hippies, flower-people. I don't know what you'd call them. But some of them took drugs and Anna joined them. Quite wild parties, they had, sometimes going on all night.'

'But what about Neal? Did he join them?'

It seemed so unlikely, knowing him now.

'I told you, he wasn't here. Anna was pregnant and that didn't please her. I often wonder whether it was Neal's baby though. She was staying with his family on the other side of the town. And then one day she disappeared. No one worried at first. She was always with that hippy group. But when a body was washed up near Aldburgh, it was identified as Anna's.'

'And she was drowned?'

'That's what the coroner said. Drowned whilst under the influence of drink and drugs. It tore Neal apart. And yet, he hardly knew her really. They'd been together for such a short time.'

'Poor Neal,' Clare said slowly.

'It all happened five or more years ago now. Life goes on, my dear. Neal's wounds have healed.'

'I quite thought he'd been divorced.'

She tried to remember just what she'd said to him, when she'd wrongly assumed that was the reason. Her words could have been so thoughtless.

But why had he never told her?

And were those wounds really healed?

★ ★ ★

The following day was Saturday and she'd promised to spend it with Nicky and John, arriving early at their tiny terraced cottage in one of the main streets of the town.

Nicola gave her an enthusiastic welcome, hugging and kissing her as if she'd been away for months, even though she'd seen her the previous evening.

'Now you must have a grand tour of the house,' she said, tucking Clare's arm through hers. 'John's worked tremendously hard ever since we returned from our honeymoon, haven't you, darling?'

John, looking chubbier than when Clare had last seen him at the wedding, bent to drop a kiss on his wife's upswept hair.

'Well, you can't do much, can you, darling — not in your condition.'

'Condition?'

Clare stared at her cousin, her eyes moving over the slender figure.

'Oh, John! It was to be my surprise. You would let it out,' Nicola pouted.

'You're pregnant? Already?' Clare asked.

'I think so, but for goodness sake don't tell Mum yet. She fusses so. I'll be flat on my back resting every day if she discovers too soon and we're not even certain yet.'

She gave a chuckle.

'And as for that gasp of 'already', I know what you're thinking, Clare, but it's not like that at all. It'll be a honeymoon baby.'

A flush of colour rose up her neck and over her cheeks as her husband murmured in her ear, 'Not that it's so surprising — considering we hardly got out of bed for the whole week.'

'Really, John! You're embarrassing Clare,' Nicola protested.

'Oh, I'm sure she's heard much worse in her job,' he grinned.

It was a tiny house, very old, but already Clare could see the improvements John had made, fitting out the kitchen with a modern round sink and units, emulsioning the walls in most of the rooms and now beginning to install fitted wardrobes.

'You certainly have been busy,' Clare enthused, stepping over a couple of boxes to enter their bedroom.

'I wouldn't have got so far without Neal's help — he's been invaluable,' commented John, running his hand cautiously down the corner of one unit to make sure it was standing squarely.

At the sound of that name, Clare felt

her heartbeat quicken and was aware of Nicola's grey eyes watching her thoughtfully.

'Everyone who steps over the threshold has to work, Clare, so watch out. John's a terrible slave-driver.'

'What can I do then?'

'Nicky's just finished making some curtains for the spare room. Do you think you could hang them? I don't want her standing on ladders.'

'Oh John! For goodness sake! You're as bad as Mum.'

'Of course I'll help. Where are they?'

She was meticulously hooking the prettily-flowered cotton onto the curtain rail, stretching up to reach as she balanced on a small pair of aluminium steps, when she heard the door open behind her and two arms closed round her waist.

'Let me do that. It's far too high for you.'

Her fingers trembled, nearly dropping the heavy curtain, and she twisted round to find herself for once looking down on the top of Neal's dark head.

Remembering their last meeting, she wasn't quite sure what his reaction would be.

'So you couldn't keep away,' he grinned, a teasing glint in his eyes. 'I didn't realise I was quite so irresistible.'

His hands still held her waist as he stepped onto the ladder, taking the curtain from her and leaning over her shoulder, continuing hooking it to the rail.

She stood quite still, feeling the pressure of his body on hers, wanting to turn her head and meet his lips, but frightened of what would happen if she did.

His heart was beating steadily, throbbing against the thin cotton of her tee-shirt, in rhythm with her own.

When the last hook was fastened, he didn't move away, his head lowering to bury itself in the fragrance of her auburn hair, one hand turning her face as his lips moved slowly across her cheek towards her mouth.

'Coffee?'

Nicola bounced into the room and stopped, staring up at them in surprise.

'Oh dear, should I have knocked?'

They both stepped down, looking embarrassed, neither of them daring to meet Nicola's laughing eyes.

'Maybe you don't want coffee,' she said.

'Of course we do,' Clare replied quickly. 'Neal was helping me reach the final hook.'

'Of course he was,' Nicola grinned. 'He knows just what a helpless kind of girl you are.'

'Can you give me a hand with these drawers, Neal,' John shouted from the next room. 'They've all gone in all right, but none of them will come out again.'

* * *

It was late that afternoon when Neal suggested a walk along the cliffs. Nicola insisted she was far too exhausted to go and John wouldn't leave her on her own, so in the end Clare was the only one left without an excuse.

The wind blowing across thick tussocks of grass was warm and the sun low in the sky, sending out long shafts of flame-coloured radiance across the foam-flecked green of the sea.

'I owe you an apology, Neal.'

'An apology? What for? I was the one to ignore you at that conference. It was very childish of me, I know, but seeing you there with that man made me angry.'

He gave her a rueful smile.

'To be quite honest, I was jealous.'

'There was no need to be, Neal.'

'It was still a stupid thing to do. What must you have thought of me?'

'Let's forget it, shall we? And anyway, I'm the one who owes you an apology.'

Clare suddenly was at a loss for words, not knowing quite how to put it.

'I'm sorry about your wife, Neal.'

His body stiffened, his eyes distant.

'I had no idea. I thought you were divorced.'

'It was a long time ago,' he said quietly.

'Tell me about her.'

'About Anna? There's not a lot to tell. I hardly knew her.'

'But you loved her?'

'Yes,' he answered. 'I loved her.'

His eyes met hers, hard and bitter.

'But she didn't love me.'

Clare reached out to touch his hand and found her fingers clasped tightly in his.

'And yet I was desperate to marry her. She was captivating. Totally desirable. A faery creature. A mermaid luring every man to his doom. I knew I wasn't the only one, and yet she chose me. I've often wondered why.'

'Maybe she did love you,' Clare said softly.

'Anna didn't know the meaning of the word. Not the true meaning. She had no idea what caring meant. The need to be with someone for always.

Never to be parted.'

His eyes looked bruised as he stared down at her, lost in the depths of his sadness.

'Anna's idea of love was possessing and being possessed, a fleeting sensation, to be repeated when and with whom she fancied. She was very young. Far too young to be married, but that was my fault. I should have known.'

A gull hovered low, poised on the wind, its wings silent as it drifted over them. Neal watched its flight until it dipped away beneath the edge of the cliff.

'If I hadn't married her, she'd still be alive. But I did, and brought her here, thinking she'd change. And here she met the people who eventually caused her death — and that of our child. If only I hadn't married her . . . '

The path in front of them ended in a crumble of earth and sand, falling away shrouded with a mesh of wire, and they turned, tracing their steps back again.

'What happened about that case you

were working on? The battered child?' Neal asked abruptly.

'Jamie Francis? He's still in care. Geoffrey's dealing with the case now and firmly convinced Tracy's boyfriend is the villain. I'm not so sure though . . . '

'Presumably Jamie has been examined by a hospital? X-rays, that sort of thing. Did they find old damage to the bones?'

'I don't know. Why? What are you suggesting?'

'Brittle bones. I read up a couple of cases after you spoke to me on the telephone. The slightest touch or fall could produce the same effect. Unaccountable fractures. It's worth suggesting.'

'I'll mention it to Geoffrey when I get back.'

Voices were coming towards them and they saw John and Nicky, arms entwined, approaching.

'So you decided to come out after all,' Clare called out.

'Well,' Nicky laughed. 'We decided that as we're an old married couple we really ought to be chaperoning you two — especially after what I saw on that ladder earlier today.'

'She's just a spoil-sport,' John protested, hugging her. 'I told her she should be encouraging you, not playing gooseberry. After all, where would we be if you'd done that to us, Neal?'

9

It seemed almost like a coincidence but soon after she returned on Monday, a message was phoned through to the office and as Geoffrey was away for a few days, it was given to Clare.

Young Jamie Francis had fractured his arm while still in care.

The news, although sad, filled her with happiness.

As they hadn't been allowed anywhere near him, there was no way Trace or Dave could have done it.

Clare immediately put in a request for tests to be made.

Days later a report was sent.

The child suffered mildly from brittle bones — just like Neal had suggested.

Clare could have danced with joy. Tracy would get her son back. It would mean she'd have to be taught how to take special care of him, but at least she could be kept under expert supervision, and the little boy and his mother would be together again.

All Clare hoped was that the separation had not caused too much trauma for both of them.

She decided to go round to tell Tracy the good news personally.

★   ★   ★

The tangled overgrown garden of the old house was almost tidy, the wrecked cars gone, its long grass trimmed down and the borders dug so that shrubs and bushes could now be seen. A blaze of orange marigolds and nasturtiums bloomed in a tub by the steps leading up to the door.

Propped against the front of the building was a ladder and Clare saw Dave rubbing away at the peeling paintwork of one of the windows.

Seeing her coming up the path, he began to climb down, his face set and grim as if preparing for trouble.

'It's good news, Dave,' she called to him, while he wiped his hands down the sides of his jeans. 'Only I want to tell Tracy first.'

'Will we get the nipper back?'

The young man's dark face had changed to eagerness now.

'All being well, any day now.'

'That's great!' he whooped.

There was no concealing the genuine sound of joy in his voice.

'Trace'll be over the moon.'

'Have you been doing all the work on this place?' Clare asked, climbing the steep wooden stairs and noticing they were no longer strewn with litter.

Dave nodded. 'The landlord's paying me to do up the whole terrace. He's made me a sort of live-in caretaker. I have to keep everything tidy, make sure it's clean, that sort of thing. The council's been on to him about the state the buildings are in. I think it put the wind up him a bit. There was some talk of compulsory purchase.'

They'd reached the top of the stairs

and Dave opened the door of their room to reveal Tracy sitting miserable in one corner, watching the television. He went across and gave her a hug.

'The lady from the solicitors has come with some news, Trace.'

Her pale pinched little face showed no emotion. She looked drained of any life.

'Jamie's fractured his arm, Tracy,' Clare explained.

The girl's expression changed, her huge eyes widening and filling with tears.

'Is it bad, miss?'

'No, nothing drastic, Tracy, but the hospital did some tests and discovered he has brittle bones. Do you under-stand what this means?'

The girl stared at her blankly. Quite obviously she didn't.

'It proves you didn't hurt him, Tracy. Whenever he fell, or even if you caught hold of him and he pulled away, it would cause damage,' Clare said gently.

'I told you, miss. I told you I never

hurt him, didn't I?'

Her voice was thin and flat, resigned, almost toneless.

'Yes, Tracy. You told me. But we had to find out the truth, didn't we? If you had been hurting him, we couldn't let it go on, could we? It wouldn't have been fair to Jamie.'

'I wouldn't never hurt my Jamie, miss. I love him too much for that.'

Tears were brimming in the girl's eyes now, slowly rolling down her thin cheeks in a steady relentless stream. Dave's arm went protectively round her shoulders and he kissed the top of her head, awkwardly stroking her cheek to brush away the tears.

'Does that mean we can see him again?' he asked, turning an anxious face to Clare. 'It's torn her apart, not seeing him.'

'I hope so. I'll get in touch with the Social Services and see what we can do.'

'I told you I never hurt him,' Tracy kept repeating monotonously, over and over again, the tears still falling.

Clare left, feeling her own eyes begin to prick as she saw the young man trying to soothe the sobbing girl, his face full of concern.

What have we done to her, she thought. What on earth have we done to that poor little thing?

*   *   *

'Mrs Poulton's divorce is tomorrow, Clare. I want you to handle it for me,' Geoffrey told her a few days later.

'Must I? You know how I feel about Mrs Poulton.'

'We can't pick and choose our clients, Clare,' he said sharply. 'Oh, and by the way, I'm thinking of taking on a new legal executive — which is why I shan't be available tomorrow. I shall be interviewing her then. A Miss Fiona Thomson. Have you ever met her? That should ease your workload a little, I hope.'

Clare certainly knew Fiona. They'd

been at Guildford together when they did their legal training. A tall, very striking girl, with wings of shining dark hair that fell round her face.

A great feeling of relief flooded through her. Maybe she wasn't going to have to worry about Geoffrey any more. Maybe it wasn't only her workload that would lose its pressure, she thought, searching out the Poulton file and beginning to study it carefully.

Mervin Poulton had moved from the district and now lived in Suffolk, she noticed. It was strange how that county seemed to crop up all the time — or was it because she'd suddenly become far more aware that it existed?

Dialling a number, she began to speak to his wife, giving her precise instructions where they should meet the next day, and the time.

'Why isn't Mr Williams going to be there?'

'I'm afraid he's tied up on another case,' Clare explained.

She couldn't very well say he was

interviewing a far more attractive female and had his own idea of priority.

'But I've been seeing Mr Williams for months now. He knows all that's happened. He understands things. I prefer to have him rather than an inexperienced lady solicitor.'

'I'm sorry, Mrs Poulton, but these things happen. I can assure you I am not inexperienced and that I am fully conversant with your case, so there's no need to worry. It should be quite straightforward.'

'Straightforward! That's where you're quite wrong, young lady. My case is extremely complicated. You ask Mr Williams.'

'Just make sure you're at court by ten forty-five, Mrs Poulton,' Clare said firmly. 'We don't want to create a bad impression by being late, do we?'

Why Geoffrey couldn't postpone his interview to a different time, she couldn't imagine — or perhaps he wanted to avoid dealing with Mrs Poulton. Some of his clients seemed to be passed over to her very frequently and none of them were the pleasant ones.

* * *

'That woman won't be in there, will she?' was the first question to greet Clare when she reached the law courts and saw Mrs Poulton waiting for her on the stone steps outside.

'Possibly. I've no idea. Does it matter?'

'I refuse to be in the same room with her,' came the flat reply.

'I'm afraid you'll have no choice,' Clare answered.

'There's no way . . . ' Mrs Poulton began, but Clare was already hurrying her along the corridor.

'In here,' she said, opening a door, and then stopped dead, the blood draining out of her face when she saw Neal sitting there, talking to a nervous-looking man and pretty young girl.

This had to be the worst moment in

her life. Meeting Neal in court, on opposing sides — and with a client like Mrs Poulton too.

His eyes flickered upwards, and for a second she thought he was about to smile, then his face became impassive when he rose to his feet.

'I understand your client, the respondent, will not agree to any of the terms proposed by my client, the petitioner,' he observed, consulting the notes before him.

'That I won't,' snapped Mrs Poulton, glaring aggressively at her husband. 'There's no way I'm agreeing to anything *she* wants, the grasping little bitch.'

'Everything must be conducted through your solicitor, Mrs Poulton,' Neal told her gently. 'She will then discuss it with you so that we can come to an amicable agreement.'

A rush of colour flooded Mrs Poulton's face, her pale eyes quickly turning to where her husband sat, holding the young girl's hand.

'My client cannot agree to the terms as they stand,' Clare said, looking deep into Neal's eyes, hating the formality surrounding them.

He was so distant, so professional. They might never have met before.

'It would save a great deal of time, if she could. My client wishes to marry again and therefore needs to sell the matrimonial home to purchase one in the area where he's now living, dividing the proceeds of sale equally between him and his former wife.'

'Equally!' snorted Mrs Poulton. 'Half each! And what sort of hovel would I be able to buy with that kind of money, may I ask?'

'There are no children,' Neal continued, 'therefore your client has no reason to retain the matrimonial home solely for herself. I think an order will be made in the terms my client desires.'

'Does he mean it's a put-up job?' Mrs Poulton hissed into Clare's ear.

'Of course not, Mrs Poulton. But it is far easier if we can agree the terms amicably so that when we go into court an order can be made stating them, without taking up the court's time arguing the point.'

'I intend to fight whatever he wants. I know my rights. That woman took him away from me and not satisfied with that, she now wants me to be a pauper. Look at her. Young enough to be his daughter. I told you he was obsessed by sex, didn't I?'

Clare tried to convince her she was not likely to win, but Mrs Poulton was having none of that.

* * *

In the end she presented such a hostile appearance that the court made an order in favour of Mervin Poulton for the marital home to be sold and the money divided equally, with a very small lump-sum payment by him to his former wife instead of maintenance.

It was also pointed out that Mrs Poulton, being still a young and active woman, should find herself suitable employment as soon as possible.

'That's what I get for having an inexperienced girl represent me in court,' Mrs Poulton observed bitterly as they left the room. 'It just goes to show, doesn't it? Men prefer to deal with their own sort and that solicitor of Mervin's certainly came over very well. I shall appeal, of course, and I don't want your firm doing it for me. Where does that other solicitor come from? The nice-looking man on Mervin's side?'

'You can't use him, I'm afraid, Mrs Poulton. He isn't allowed to act for both the respondent and the petitioner. And anyway, he lives in Suffolk.'

Mrs Poulton stalked down the steps, her high heels clattering loudly, her face set in a tight mask of fury.

'Well, there's no way I want you to represent me, thank you, young lady. I'll make quite sure I see Mr Williams next time. I can't think what he was at, sending a chit of a girl like you. I knew right away I was on the losing side.

Stuck out plain as the nose on your face, that did. Doomed, right from the start. It's a man's job.'

Clare stood, watching her, and pushed her thick auburn hair wearily away from her aching forehead.

What a terrible display she'd made in court, and in front of Neal too. Unable to control her client who kept voicing her opinion loudly; presenting the case in a stammering, disorganised manner; then ending up with such a poor result.

A hand touched her shoulder.

'I'm sorry I had to do that to you,' Neal apologised, 'but we're all out to get the best for our clients, aren't we?'

Clare nodded glumly.

'What a woman! You really didn't stand much chance, Clare, did you? She blackened her case with every word she uttered. And, of course, Mervin came over so well as the henpecked and over-dominated husband. He gained the immediate sympathy of the court.'

'She is dreadful — a typical example

206

of a woman scorned. You can see why he left her,' Clare said. 'I'm glad she lost out.'

'Really, Clare! How unprofessional.'

That teasing smile was curving his lips upwards at the corners, making her skin tingle.

'No, how about a meal? I'm not travelling back to Suffolk until the morning. Or will your lover object?'

'My lover?'

'That aggressive man who was so attentive to you the last time we met.'

'Geoffrey?'

She laughed.

'I should really let him know what's happened, it's his case. But it can wait until tomorrow.'

He was probably already dining the beautiful Fiona.

* * *

While they were eating, she told him about Jamie.

'I'm glad you managed to sort things

out satisfactorily. It was upsetting you, wasn't it?'

Clare eased a stone from the cherry on her grapefruit.

'Tracy Francis loves the child so much. It was so obvious. I couldn't see how she'd be able to hurt him, but there was her background — a father who'd beaten his own children. It becomes the pattern of life. I feel so sorry for her. The whole thing affected her badly. She's like a zombie now. Totally lost and confused.'

Neal's hand closed over hers.

'You did what you could. You couldn't do more.'

'Couldn't I? Why didn't I think of getting the hospital to do tests right at the beginning? If I had, Jamie would never have been taken away in the first place. Tracy would have been spared all that trauma. I should have known.'

'What about Geoffrey? You said he'd taken the case over, didn't you? He should have known, rather than you. He's been in the profession far longer.'

'I'm a total failure, Neal. First Jamie, then that Poulton woman. You were right. There's no way I can do the job properly. Look at me now, drained by all the emotion.'

'Come and live in Suffolk and marry me instead.'

She sighed. If only she could say yes, but still her stubborn pride wouldn't let her give in.

When they said goodbye outside her flat, Clare was tempted to invite him in, but if she did, she knew she might weaken. After such an exhausting day, all she wanted now was a shower before sinking into the depths of a good night's sleep.

Neal brushed her cheek with his lips and she wondered sadly just how much longer he would bother with her.

* * *

As she came in the door and switched on the light, it clicked but nothing more.

'Oh, damn. The bulb's gone.'

She made her way across the room cautiously, trying not to bump into any furniture or ladder her tights — one of the more expensive items in her wardrobe as they seemed to constantly get snagged on something every day.

A faint illumination came in through the window from the streetlights outside and she could vaguely make out the outline of the table as she passed, stumbling her way towards the bedroom.

When she went to open it, the door was slightly ajar and yet she was quite sure she had closed it behind her that morning. She had a thing about leaving doors open, remembering her father's frequent protest in her childhood: 'Weren't born in a tent, were you, Clare?'

The hand that snapped over her mouth was rough and powerful with a faint smell of vinegar and chips on the fingers.

She tried to breathe, but terror had

robbed her of that ability, almost suffocating her with panic.

'Hullo, gorgeous. You ain't half kept me waiting.'

Ed Booker's voice was unmistakable, as was the cold pressure of the thin-bladed knife he held against her neck.

Slowly he slid his fingers away from her lips, pushing the knife more closely into her skin.

'One sound, gorgeous, and your carpet's ruined for ever.'

Her throat felt dry and her breath rasped as she tried to swallow, gasping for air.

'But you're in prison,' she managed to force out painfully.

'Got a double then, ain't I?'

Ed gave a mirthless chuckle.

'How did you escape?'

'Easy. Me mum's funeral. Had to attend, didn't I? Really cut up, I was. Stupid old cow.'

He chuckled again.

'Right out in the country, we were.

Stupid place for a crematorium. All woods and things. Stupid copper felt sorry for me. Young chap. Nearly sobbing himself, he was. Undid me cuffs. That's when I legged it.'

He gave a short laugh and the knife quivered.

'You didn't . . . ' Clare began, then hesitated not really wanting to know.

'Top him? Dunno. Gave him a jab with me knife. Green as grass, he was. Didn't even check me over, did he? Asking for trouble.'

'I always knew you were a villain.'

Clare's voice was strong now, venting her anger.

'Got something right for once then, have you? Makes up for that little balls-up of yours in court, doesn't it?'

'Well,' said Clare, attempting a bluff, 'what are we going to do now? I don't intend to stand here like this all night and in any case your wrist's going to get a bit tired in a minute. Shall we put on the light and sit down properly?'

The knife pricked into her neck.

'No way, gorgeous. What do we need lights for?'

His arm was already wavering slightly.

'I'm starving,' Clare lied, trying not to remember the steak she'd recently eaten. 'How about you?'

'I could do with a bite,' Ed said slowly. 'No tricks though.'

'No tricks,' she promised, feeling the knife move away. 'Look, Ed. I'll have to put the light on before I can make a meal for you.'

'A sandwich'll do.'

'Even so . . . '

Her hand reached out towards the switch but before she could press it, there was a sharp ring at the doorbell.

Instantly Ed's arm was back round her neck, the knife hard against her skin.

'I'll have to answer it.'

'Shut up!' he hissed.

The bell rang again.

'Clare. Are you all right? Why haven't you put any lights on? Have they fused or something?'

213

It was Neal.

Clare's heart gave a leap of joy until she realised the danger they would both be in if he tried to come inside.

'It's one of my neighbours,' she lied.

'Make an excuse. Tell him to go away,' Ed growled, tightening his grip on her.

'Clare!'

'Sorry, Mark. You woke me. I was sound asleep. I've been in bed for hours.'

Silence echoed round her. Would Neal understand? She was terrified he'd make some comment about the name she'd used or the obvious lie.

'Are you quite sure you're all right, Clare? I think I'd better come in.'

The knife was pressing harder into her throat.

'Not now, Mark. It's late. I'm feeling a bit under the weather. Probably that bug you had a week or so ago.'

'Okay then. I'll be seeing you.'

Had he emphasised those final words? Ed let his arm slide away and she slumped, her legs suddenly feeling weak and useless.

'Pity you couldn't put on a performance like that when I came up in court,' Ed muttered darkly while she opened the fridge, and in the light from it, took out some ham and bread to make a sandwich.

'What now?' she asked, hearing the unpleasant noise as he bit into it and began to chew open-mouthed. 'The police are sure to be looking for you.'

'Not in here they aren't.'

'Can I put a light on? I hate this darkness.'

'If you want, but we shan't be here much longer.'

Clare wasn't sure whether the brightness was a comfort or not, seeing Ed standing there in front of her, cramming in the food. He wasn't a pretty sight and now she could see the vicious-looking knife he held, almost lovingly, in his hand, one finger gently caressing its evil-looking blade.

'Got a car?'

Clare shook her head.

'I don't drive.'

'Have to take one then, won't we?'

'We? Why do you need to take me?'

'Insurance. That's what you are. Won't shoot while you're around, will they?'

'Where are you going?'

'Got a mate with a boat down near Worthing. He owes me a favour. Get moving.'

Ed pushed her towards the door and opened it cautiously. The corridor was empty.

Catching hold of her arm, with the knife digging into her side, Ed hurried along the passage, his pig-like eyes darting nervously from side to side.

Where was Neal? Surely he realised something was wrong. Why wasn't he there to rescue her?

Clare expected any second he'd leap out and overpower Ed, but when they reached the street, she began to despair.

Cars were parked all the way along. Within seconds Ed had the door of an old Ford Fiesta undone and with a jab of the knife, pushed her inside, across the seat.

At least he can't drive and hold the knife at the same time, she thought with a slight feeling of relief. Maybe she could undo the door as they went along, but the speed with which he raced through the darkened streets soon dissuaded her from that idea.

Her eyes glanced at the petrol gauge. With any luck it would read empty.

It didn't; the needle pointed to well over three-quarters full — enough to get the sixty miles or so to Worthing without any trouble.

Why hadn't Neal done anything? All it took was a 999 call and the police should be pursuing them rapidly, but the roads seemed almost deserted.

What would happen when they got to Worthing? Would Ed abandon her and speed off abroad somewhere in his friend's boat?

Or would he kill her?

Another unpleasant thought began to worry her.

Suppose the police were following and used guns?

A bullet striking Ed would probably result in the car crashing at speed. And one hitting her could kill.

Either way she didn't stand much chance.

They had left the built-up, well-lit streets behind now, passing through Kingston, over Kew Bridge, racing past Chessington Zoo, woodland and open country flashing by the windows.

She remembered her father taking her to the zoo, oh years ago now. It had been winter, a faint gleam of frost patterning the grass.

'Smell's not so bad at this time of year,' he explained.

There'd been a thin black bear in a cage and as she skipped along, it had followed her movements. She skipped back again and the bear followed her again.

'It's a dancing bear, Daddy,' she'd cried, but he wasn't listening, his eyes following the bottom of a slender jeans-clad girl pushing a small child in a buggy.

The pond was frozen where the penguins lived, but her father said they'd probably been born at the zoo, so they wouldn't even know it was like their own homeland. They'd slithered and slipped and didn't seem to be very good at walking on ice at all, which she thought very strange.

She'd wanted to go to the fair over on the far side of the field. One of the girls at school had been there once and told everyone all about it, but her father said it wasn't open in the winter.

The visit had been quite a disappointment, because most of the animals had been hiding at the back of their cages or buried deep in heaps of straw, trying to keep warm.

* * *

The speedometer showed well beyond ninety and Ed's foot was flat against the floor.

'You'll get caught for speeding,' Clare warned, her law-abiding instinct overcoming her fear.

Ed gave a snort of laughter.

'That's the least of me worries, gorgeous.'

They were on the new stretch of the A24 bypassing Horsham now, the sky above clear and star-bright, a full moon outlining sheep in the fields like pale ghosts.

'What are you going to do with me?' she had to ask, her voice trembling.

Ed kept his eyes on the road ahead, his knuckles gleaming white as they gripped the steering-wheel.

'You know where I'm going, don't you?'

'No, I don't,' Clare protested quickly. 'How can I? All you've told me is you have a friend with a boat near Worthing.'

'So that means crossing the Channel, don't it?'

'Does it?' She tried to sound vague.

'So as soon as I dumped you, you'd

tell the Old Bill, wouldn't you and they'd cover every bit of coast on both sides.'

'They're going to catch up with you eventually, Ed, wherever you are.'

'Why should they? Others do it. The continent's full of villains,' Ed retorted confidently. 'They do programmes about them on telly. Heroes, they are. And films. Think of that bloke who robbed a train.'

'You'll get a really stiff sentence when they do catch you. Why not give yourself up now and make it a bit easier?'

'So's you can stand up in court and defend me again? Not likely. I'd probably get the rope with you around. No, I'm off to start a new life.'

'And what about your family and friends in England?'

'What family and friends?' he sneered. 'Me dad's inside and me mum's gone up in smoke — not that she's ever done me much good. Lit off with some bloke when I was a little kid.'

'What about brothers and sisters?'

'Me brother Andy's inside too and as for me sister . . . she's been on the game since she was eleven. That's me dad for you. Pimping out his own kid.' Ed's voice was full of bitterness.

Clare almost felt sorry for him. What chance had he had? What future did he have? Maybe it was best that he did go abroad and try to make a new start. At least it would give him a chance of making good.

'What will you do — if you do get away?' she asked.

'Just think of the pickings over there. All them wealthy tourists! Pockets bulging.'

'Oh Ed, I despair of you!'

They were in Findon Valley now on the final run into Worthing, rows of bungalows and houses bordering the road.

Ahead of them in the glare of the tall overhanging streetlights, Clare saw a vast cemetery bordered by the stumps of hurricane-shattered trees, its rows of tombstones, grey, flowers drooping.

And beside it was a roundabout — with police cars blocking every road leading away from it.

10

The bright iridescent orange and yellow lines along their sides glowed in the streetlights.

Ed slowed the Fiesta, wrenching it round with a desperate twist, tyres screeching as it slewed sideways. For a terrifying second the engine stalled, then roared into life again as the car headed back the way it had come, first houses, then trees and hedges racing past.

At the next roundabout, at the top of an incline, Ed swung the steering-wheel sharply to the left and began to chuckle.

'That showed 'em.'

'They'll set up another roadblock, you know,' Clare warned.

'It'll take a while for them to get there.'

'I dare say they have several more

cars dotted round the district, not just that lot,' Clare pointed out drily.

'They'll need 'em to catch up with me.'

Eventually they met the A27 at high speed and Ed turned the wheel in a frantic attempt to turn the corner, the front of the car ending up on the grass verge.

The engine revved wildly as the wheels spun uselessly, spatters of mud flying up into the air around them, before finally gripping the edge of the road again and the car bounced back onto the tarmac with a bone-jarring jolt.

Clare felt for the lock with desperate questing fingers. Now was the time to escape, before the car gained speed again, but even as the door yawned open, Ed's hand shot out, grabbing her, jerking her back inside with a sickening wrench.

The door slammed shut, trapping the sleeve of her jacket, and she winced at the thought that it could so easily have been her arm.

Not that Ed would have cared.

'Try that again, gorgeous,' he snarled through clenched teeth and she saw the glint of the knife in his hand.

They were travelling down a narrow, winding, wooded lane, meeting each sharp bend with a scream of tyres. Clare lurched from side to side in the seat, her arm still held against the door, trying in vain to free the material from it.

Sobs were choking her throat and her eyes stung with frantically held-back tears. If only she'd acted more quickly. She felt furious with herself for such a slow reaction. Couldn't she do anything right?

The lane ended, meeting a major road, and they shot across another roundabout, seeing ahead of them flashing red lights as the arm of a barrier began its descent.

'What the hell?'

'It's a level-crossing,' Clare shouted. 'For God's sake stop, Ed!'

The car seemed to rise into the air,

bouncing high over the rails, and there was a shuddering crash on the metal roof as the barrier hit it.

They were clear, hearing the roar and rattle of the train as it hurtled across behind them in a blaze of lighted windows, faces peering out at the sudden noise.

Closing her eyes, Clare leaned against the seat, tasting blood on her bitten lips.

Ed was laughing again, a high-pitched sound that grated on her nerves. She began to wonder if it was hysteria or whether he was high on drugs.

WORTHING 2 glowed on a signpost as they tore past the sleeping houses.

'It's somewhere round here,' Ed muttered, slowing the car.

He wound down the window and Clare could smell the sharp salt smell of the sea.

A row of lights sparkled in the far distance and she guessed it was a pier. Others glinted here and there on the darkness of the sea where boats were fishing.

She could hear the pounding of waves thud against the shore.

'Have you been here before?' she asked Ed.

'A couple of times,' he grunted.

The car wheels crunched over gravel and from somewhere nearby came the metallic rattle of steel ropes against masts.

Ed stopped the car and listened, his head leaning through the open window.

'Mick goes fishing most nights. He keeps his boat somewhere her. Get out.'

The wind was cold, biting into her face and lifting her hair from the warmth of her neck. Clare tried to huddle down into her thin jacket. A cotton suit wasn't the thing to be wearing on a beach in the early hours of the morning.

With a jerk of her arm, Ed pulled her forward, peering closely at the boats hauled up onto the pebbles.

'They all look the same to me,' he growled.

Clare stumbled, one high-heeled shoe twisting sideways on the stones. A shaft of agony shot through her ankle and she cried out in pain.

Instantly the knife was at her throat, Ed's pale face thrust close to hers.

'Shut up!' he hissed. 'D'you want everyone to hear you?'

'I've twisted my ankle,' Clare gasped, gritting her teeth in agony.

'Too bad! Get them shoes off before you do it again.'

She winced, kicking off her other shoe and feeling the sharpness of the pebbles beneath her feet.

'This is it!' Ed's whisper was triumphant. '*Mighty Mouse.* Clever that, ain't it?'

Clare stared back at him blankly in the growing light.

'Mick. That's his name. Mickey Mouse. *Mighty Mouse.* Get it?'

Ed jerked her arm viciously, jarring her body right down to her toes.

229

Clare nodded, wondering exactly what he intended to do now he'd found the boat. It wasn't large. Surely he couldn't hope to cross the Channel in that?

Did he have any idea of how to sail it, or even in which direction to go?

Lights flickered behind them as a car edged its way slowly into the car-park. Clare turned her head.

Broad bands of colour glowed along its white sides, the headlights beaming out to reach the dark seaweed-strewn edge of the shoreline.

Like an eel she squirmed her body sideways, wriggling out of Ed's grasp, and trying to ignore the jagged pain of her ankle, stumbled, frantically shouting, over the uneven ground.

Car doors opened and then slammed. Two uniformed figures were moving rapidly towards her.

The pain tore through her ankle like fire.

They were only yards away. She had to reach them.

Her throat ached in the cold night air.

Only feet away now.

Ed's fingers tangled into her hair, dragging her head back, the knife biting into the soft skin of her neck. Clare felt a sudden warmth seep downwards to the silky collar of her blouse.

She stood quite still.

The policemen had stopped too.

Ed was walking backwards now, slowly, very slowly, dragging her with him.

One stumble, one false step, and Clare knew the knife would slice cleanly through her throat. Even now her skin burned and stung with its sharpness.

'Let her go!' The words were a command.

Clare lifted heavy eyes to stare at the policeman's face. He looked so young, fresh-faced and eager, far too young to know how to deal with such a situation.

The dawn was growing now, long fingers of flame inching up over the horizon, turning the sea to a glow of orange radiance.

A blackbird sang in the feathery fronds of a tamarisk bush, the notes rippling through the silent air.

Somewhere she could hear the clatter of a milk-float.

'Let her go.'

This time it came more quietly and she let her gaze travel to the second man, older, thickset and ruddy-faced, his hair slightly greying.

She could feel the blood on her neck soaking into her collar, the warmth turning to an unpleasant chill.

The policemen's faces blurred.

I mustn't faint, pulsed the message in her brain.

'Give me the knife, son.'

He had a kindly voice, like a patient father talking to a child, firm but still kindly.

'Give it to him, Ed,' she whispered, her lips hardly able to form the words.

Even that slight movement made the blood gush, spreading over Ed's shaking fingers. She heard the sudden intake of his breath and the slight moan, feeling his grip slacken.

Then they both fainted.

★   ★   ★

The doctor at the hospital was brusque.

'Merely a graze,' he observed calmly, when she flinched from the sting of antiseptic. 'It won't need stitching. That ankle's badly sprained though. We'll need to strap it.'

Neal drove her back. He'd suddenly appeared in the curtained recess, his handsome face drained of all colour, his dark eyes anguished.

'Oh, Clare!'

His arms closed round her, his mouth moving to meet hers.

'Gently,' laughed the young black nurse. 'She's already in a state of shock.'

'What kept you?' Clare whispered with a hint of humour.

'They wouldn't let me join the chase. After all I'd told them too.'

His fingers were caressing her cheek.

'They were following you all the way.

Close behind. It was too dangerous, they said, to jump him.'

Clare felt the movement of his hand cease for a second.

'I've been waiting, going out of my mind, imagining what could be happening. And then, eventually, they phoned me.'

His eyes were smiling down at her, with a glimmer of their old familiar teasing.

'I'm going to need a good solicitor to deal with my speeding summonses. Do you think you'll be up to that?'

'You'd still want me to do that — with my track record?' she whispered, wincing at the pull on her neck as she tried to smile back at him.

'Oh, I still want you,' he replied, his lips brushing an auburn curl resting on her cheek. 'I'll always want you, Clare.'

★   ★   ★

On the journey back, Clare leaned her head against the tweed of his jacket, her shaking body now still, feeling safe at last.

'All those questions,' he growled angrily. 'Why couldn't the police have waited? All I want to do is get you home.'

Her eyes closed and didn't open again until they were slowing to a halt outside a tall Victorian house by a smooth well-kept green, a faint smell of salt filling the soft warm air.

Clare stared, thinking she was still dreaming.

Aunt Margaret and Uncle Bill came hurrying down the path, their faces distressed.

'You poor child!' Aunt Margaret's eyes were filled with tears.

Clare looked up at Neal, bewildered.

'I told you I was bringing you home,' he smiled.

'But . . . '

'No buts. You're home now — to stay. I'm not taking no for an answer any longer. It's quite obvious you need someone to take care of you. Really,

Clare. Going off with a strange man like that was asking for trouble. Didn't your mother ever warn you?'

She gazed into his eyes, seeing the wicked twinkle of mischief that filled them, and wanted to laugh with sheer happiness, but the strapping on her neck made it impossible.

'You'll stay here with us until the wedding, dear,' Aunt Margaret was saying as she fussed round, finding cushions and a rug to wrap round her.

'Wedding? But . . . '

Clare wondered if she was going demented. Nicky's wedding was weeks ago now.

She stared from Uncle Bill to Aunt Margaret, seeing the amused expression on their faces, then her eyes turned back to Neal.

'*Our* wedding, of course,' he declared. 'We'll make it a repeat of last time but reverse the roles. Bride and groom swapped for bridesmaid and best man. I'm sure Nicky and John will be only too pleased and I don't think it will confuse the vicar too much.'

'But . . . '

'Oh, Clare, do stop butting,' he laughed, his lips caressing the top of her head and tracing their way down to her upturned waiting mouth.

'For once in your life, you're going to succumb to some male domination for a change and do exactly what you're told.'

We do hope that you have enjoyed reading this large print book.

Did you know that all of our titles are available for purchase?

We publish a wide range of high quality large print books including:
Romances, Mysteries, Classics
General Fiction
Non Fiction and Westerns

Special interest titles available in large print are:
The Little Oxford Dictionary
Music Book, Song Book
Hymn Book, Service Book

Also available from us courtesy of Oxford University Press:
Young Readers' Dictionary
(large print edition)
Young Readers' Thesaurus
(large print edition)

For further information or a free brochure, please contact us at:
Ulverscroft Large Print Books Ltd.,
The Green, Bradgate Road, Anstey,
Leicester, LE7 7FU, England.
Tel: (00 44) 0116 236 4325
Fax: (00 44) 0116 234 0205

REGAN'S FALL

Valeric Holmes

After the death of their father and the removal of their gentle mother to debtors' prison, Regan and her brother Isaac are left in desperate circumstances. Their only hope is to appeal for aid from an estranged relative at Marram Hall, Lady Arianne, whom neither sibling has ever met. Upon her arrival, Regan encounters the handsome and masterful James Coldwell, the local magistrate, but fears that if she trusts him he will throw her and Isaac out of the house — or worse. Then Lady Arianne attempts to do just that . . .

A LITTLE LOVING

Gael Morrison

Jenny Holden fell in love with Matt Chambers, the local high school football star. When she fell pregnant, he didn't believe the baby was his. Now a pro player, he is back in town to attend the wedding of his best friend, who is also Jenny's boss. And when he sees Jenny's son Sam, the boy's parentage is unquestionable. Jenny, now a widow, knows all Sam wants is a father — his real father. But can she trust the man who once turned his back on them?

MISTS OF DARKNESS

Rebecca Bennett

Who tried to kill TV producer Zannah Edgecumbe by pushing her over a cliff? The answer is hidden somewhere in her slowly returning memory. Is it cameraman Jonathan Tyler, her aggressive and passionate fiancé, or is it Matthew Tregenna, the handsome but remote doctor treating her — the man with whom she is falling in love? She remembers Hugh, the boy she adored as a child — but where is he now? Lost in an abyss of blurred and broken memories, Zannah must return to the cliff-top to discover the horrifying truth.

A QUESTION OF LOVE

Gwen Kirkwood

As a partner in Kershaw & Co., Roseanne has very clear plans for her career and her life. She is fiercely independent, and has no time for anything outside of work — until she meets Euan Kennedy, the nephew of her business partner, Mr Kershaw. Euan is funny, warm, charming — and drop-dead gorgeous. But when Euan doubts Roseanne's integrity, the feelings that have started to grow between them are dashed. How can she ever love a man who thinks so little of her?